To Care

I hope y
enjoy

The Long Road /

End Of The Line

James Jobling

ISBN-13:
978-1973885955

ISBN-10:
1973885956

Table of contents

The Long Road

A novella

James Jobling

CHAPTER 1

That's it. Never again. I mean it this time. I've had enough. I'm sick and tired of all her demanding bullshit. I should have manned up and finished it a long time ago. Would have, too, was it not for the guillotine hovering above my head. What the hell was I thinking? Cheating on Darcy with that little sort from the Golden Wings a few months back was one thing. This, though… this is *completely* different.

For starters, Harriett Bronte isn't an eighteen-year-old bottle-blonde with more curves than the Monte Carlo racetrack. Nor does she earn a living serving pints of watery lager to the local lushes of Birmingham who believe that ogling her cleavage, jiggling her hips, or groping her backside to be a sure-fire way of getting into her underwear.

No, Harriett Bronte is *nothing* like the barmaid from the Golden Wings. In fact, Harriett – or *Mrs. Bronte* as she insists I refer to her as during office hours - is a complete different kettle of fish.

A red light is coming up in the not-so-distant-distance. I ease my foot down on the brake and bring the gurgling Honda Civic to an obedient stop. Drizzle speckles the windscreen, distorting my view of the high street to nothing more than a blurry mirage, and I switch on the wipers. The road stretching in front of me is dead. No traffic queues on either side of the junction. Hardly a surprise, though. Most people (correction; most *sane* people who choose not to cheat on their pregnant fiancée with their vindictive boss) prefer to be tucked into bed with a hot chocolate and a good book to being out in the cold and the rain. Trust me, if I had a choice, I would much rather be on the sofa with a beer and watching *Cannibal Apocalypse* than driving home from another bout of meaningless sex in a cheap hotel. Trouble is, my baby girl will be here next month, and I still have a ton of things to buy.

Pram? No. Moses basket? Not yet. Steriliser? Nada. Breast pads? What the hell are they? Baby clothes? Nappies? Formula? No. No. And, err… no. Darcy and I are far too laid back to be properly prepared. Maybe that is because we are both young, but these past eight months have virtually flown by, and we don't have any of the necessities. To get them, I need to keep my job at the Bronte & Garvin Legal Advisors and, to do that, I must degrade myself by succumbing to the lecherous demands of my forty-eight-year-old tyrant of a boss – just to get a couple of extra hundred quid in my pay-packet each month. My prostitution sickens me.

The traffic light switches from amber to green, so I put the car into gear and rumble forwards. Scintillating neon lights spill from the front windows of takeaways and burger bars lining both sides of the road, making the puddles sparkle and glimmer. From somewhere further afield, the *throb-*

throb-throb of acid-house music blares from a nightclub. To my right, a group of hooded youths are fucking around outside of a Chinese chip shop, flinging food at each other and hollering at the top of their teenage lungs. I press down harder on the accelerator when one of the vicious louts salutes me with his middle finger.

This is just one of the many things that I hate about my deceitful trysts with Harriett – having to drive through the city late at night. Probably sounds a bit childish, but it's almost like the city transforms into another world come nightfall. Parts of Birmingham turn into a jungle where only the deprived and most violent dare tread. Earlier this year, my car failed its MOT and, after indulging in another lewd session in a sleazy B&B with Harriett, I realised that I had left my wallet in the office. Not having enough cash to cover the fare of a taxi home (and not wanting to sink any further into my employer's debt); I had to make do with the bus.

You would not believe the sights of squalor and desperation that I witnessed on that journey. Every alleyway or shop doorway that we passed was crammed with down-and-outers who were huddled together in sleeping bags or sprawled on the ground under wet blankets. It was disheartening, and I did not feel great about returning to my warm home that night.

Some of the homeless in the city have barely graduated from high school. How have their lives become so twisted and warped? Why can't they just go home? What would happen if they did? And why are our government doing nothing about it? They send millions of pounds to foreign countries each year, yet refuse to bring up the subject of Britain's housing crisis within the walls of Parliament. And should somebody audaciously suggest we look after our own citizens before bailing some distant country out of debt, they get ridiculed or branded racist.

As though right on cue, the bright lights of my Honda reveal a row of tents pegged to a scrap of shrubland by the roadside. The rubber groove of my wiper squeakily clears spittle from the windscreen, and I squint at the 'camp site'; taking in a dozen plastic garden chairs circling a bonfire which has been left to burn out inside of a metal bin. I can't see anybody hunched around the fire, but I do catch a glimpse of a washing line clogged with wringing wet baby grows, roped between two tents. A child's buggy sits abandoned in the rain.

The rise in homeless people living on the streets of Birmingham is only *half* the reason why I hate driving at night. Gangs of youths - like those I passed just now outside of the chip shop - lurk beneath the shadow of night; arrogant and cocksure in the knowledge that the police refuse to regulate patrols down here anymore. Can't say I blame them much. The Mandy Moore estate, just to my right, has a reputation for being as rough as fuck.

Then there are the flat-out oddities.

I shit you not, I once saw a middle-aged man wearing overalls and an orange wig (like the man-perm that Lionel Blair rocked in his *Name That Tune* heyday), topped off with a pair of novelty sunglasses perched on his face. This weirdo was frantically pedalling a *child's* bicycle - complete with stabilisers - down the high street. One other late-night excursion led to me witnessing two drunks beating the holy crap out of each other over a dead cat! I guess it's true what they say: they only ever come out at night.

My phone starts ringing.

For a couple of seconds, I struggle to work out which phone the ringtone belongs to. Regardless of what you believe, I *do* love Darcy. The last thing I want to do is to hurt her – especially now she is carrying my daughter. That's why I've decided I'm done living this double life. First thing tomorrow morning, I intend on marching straight into Harriett Bronte's office and telling her that we are through. Finished. History. Over. Kaput. If she wants to fire my arse afterwards, she can. I don't care. I've had enough. I want to be a good father... hell, maybe even a good husband one day. From this point on, the cheating – both bribed *and* voluntary – stop. I would rather earn a crust sweeping the streets than to have to weasel a wage out of that blackmailing bitch.

It's because of her that I've *two* phones in the first place. Last thing I want is for Darcy to scroll through my phone and stumble upon a saucy text or filthy Snapchat photo that Harriett has sent (something she tends to do regularly). I have asked her not to do this on several near-miss occasions, but there's no negotiating with that mad cow. She once told me that the thought of getting caught by Darcy or her husband – that rich yank – turned her on. I don't see how. My bowels used to quiver every time I received a text or a call. That's why I had to get a cheap pay as you go Samsung – just to keep the demented witch a secret.

Vibration inside the breast pocket of my shirt fills me with relief as I realise it is my iPhone – *not* the Samsung – that's ringing. Pulling the phone out, I swipe the screen to accept the call and wedge it between my shoulder and jaw, wrapping the fingers on both hands tightly around the hard leather of the steering wheel. The carriageway leading to the motorway is fast approaching and already I can see the rear lights of cars whizzing by.

"Sweetheart," I breathe into the mouthpiece of the phone. "I'm so sorry I am late."

"Where are you?" Darcy asks from the sofa of our bungalow in Walsall.

"Nearly home," I reply as I drive past a group of heckling women staggering along on the pavement. They're soaked to the skin and blatantly pissed, wearing the traditional skimpy decor of a hen party – plastic tiaras, veils, L-plates, matching T-shirts with names like **GULPING GRANNY** emblazoned across broad backs. One of the screeching women bends over and hitches up her denim miniskirt, slapping both cheeks of her arse as she moons me. Drunken comrades cheer and applaud this. I bite my lip to avoid bursting into laughter and tell my fiancée that I should only be another twenty minutes or so.

"Okay. Drive carefully," Darcy instructs through a yawn. "It's really pouring down."

"I know." Leaving the high street in my rear-view mirror, the front wheels of the Honda cruise onto the tarmac of the ramp leading to the motorway. "You get to bed, okay? It's late."

"I may nap on the sofa. You know I can't sleep until I know you're safely home."

I clench my teeth tightly together. Fingers throttle the steering wheel as though it was Harriett Bronte's throat. Thunder grumbles overhead, but the beat of my heart throbbing within my ears dwarfs it.

"I really am sorry I'm late."

A stretch of clear ramp leads to the exit that will eventually spill onto the motorway. I slam my foot against the accelerator and burn rubber.

"No need to apologise, love. You're working late to notch up the overtime. I understand."

"Still doesn't make me feel any less of a dickhead."

"Well, don't." Darcy commands incoherently through another yawn. "You're a good man."

The Samsung in the glovebox suddenly springs to life, its cramped, holding cell only slightly muffling its ringtone. Shit, I must have forgot to turn the ringer off after our session. As the piercing jingle fills the car, I slow down, fumbling awkwardly with trembling fingers to unlatch the glovebox. Only Harriett has the number for the Samsung. It *must* be her!

The glovebox snaps open and, blindly, I delve my hand inside, rummaging amongst crumpled receipts, twisted napkins, boiled sweets, my log book, before finally finding the nuisance phone.

Grabbing it, I thumb disconnect just as Darcy asks what that noise was. My heart leaps into my throat, throbbing obnoxiously in my gullet, suffocating me. I try to swallow, but my mouth can't produce any saliva. Shit, what do I tell her? What do I say?

"Noise? Oh, you mean Rich's phone." Even *I'm* impressed with how authentic my voice sounds. Another grumble of thunder chastises from above.

"Rich? Who's *Rich?*" Darcy enquires.

"You know Rich, sweetheart. Rich Hawkins. You must have heard me mention him at least a dozen times. He's my colleague from the office. Sits right next to me and Mark Cope, does Rich. I must have brought his name up in conversation before now. Anyhow, we went to KFC for lunch and—"

"*Bruce!*" Darcy reprimands.

Straightaway, I cringe in my seat.

"What do you mean you went to KFC for lunch? You promised you'd lay off the junk food. You're going to be a dad in a few weeks, Bruce. Do you know how badly fried food clogs your arteries? Do you have a clue just how much saturated fat is in that crap?"

I blow out my cheeks and roll my eyes at the reflection in my wing mirror. And to think; I had a Caesar salad for lunch.

"I know, I know. Take it easy, babe, I only had a latte; I give you my word. Anyhow, Rich - the daft sod - only went and left his phone on the passenger seat."

I open my mouth to pile more manure onto the heap of steaming bullshit, when the phone starts ringing again. Screeching like an air-raid siren, the unexpected scream catches me by surprise, and I drop it. Ricocheting off the gear stick, the cheap Samsung lands in the footwell, right next to the accelerator pedal.

"Shit," I curse in frustration.

"What's wrong?" Darcy's innocent voice fills my ear. I had forgot that I was still holding the phone to the side of my face.

A broad flash of sheet lightning ignites the black sky. Fat raindrops splatter against the windscreen as the sulking heavens finally open. I am very close to the motorway – penned in on either side of the ramp by oblique foliage – and I can clearly see the shimmering black outlines of traffic hurtling by.

"Nothing, sweetheart," I growl into the mouthpiece of my iPhone. Switching the wipers from occasional to constant, I reduce my speed a tad. "I just dropped Rich's phone, that's all. Give you a call back once I'm off the motorway, okay?"

"Okay. Take care driving in the rain, love. I'll see you when you get home. Your dinner will probably be burnt to a crisp, but I'll make you a sandwich when you get in."

Smiling, I say farewell to Darcy and hang up. I toss the iPhone onto the empty passenger seat and, with one hand draped across the wheel; I reach into the footwell, craning my neck to one side so that I can keep a watchful eye on road. Fingertips stroke the screaming mobile and, with only seconds before

I join the throng on the motorway, I grab the shrieking phone and decline the call again, jolting back upright just as I hit her.

CHAPTER 2

I don't *know* that it's a *her*.

At this point, I don't know if I have hit *anything*.

It all happened so fast. It was far too dark to make anything of specific relevance out. All I know is that *something* rushed in front of my speeding headlamps. And that's it. The right side of my bonnet *may* have clipped whatever it had been, but I don't know. Not for certain, anyhow.

Before I can consider pulling over to check, the Honda has barrelled onto the motorway, and I am now galloping along the M6 like a racing bullet. I can't pull over here. It'd be unpractical, not to mention dangerous. I mean, it was most likely nothing serious, anyway.

There isn't much traffic on the motorway, so I *could* switch lanes and bring my car to a stop on the hard shoulder. If I *did* hit somebody – and I'm certain it was nothing more than a carrier bag caught by the wind, or a strip of rubber snatched from the mud flap of one of the eighteen wheelers that race up and down the carriageways - then there would be evidence in the form of damage sustained to the front of the car, right? A cracked headlamp. Denting to the bodywork. Maybe even blood - although the heavy rain would have probably washed any of that away. The thought of pulling my car to the side of the motorway and getting out in such Godawful weather fills me with dread. What if I was to get struck by another motorist like that American horror novelist?

My heart is plodding away like a jackhammer, and my hands are trembling uncontrollably. Another flash of lightning forks across the sky, but I pay it scant attention as the harsh beams of the headlights reveal a signpost mounted in the knee-high grass and stinging nettles on the roadside: **HAPPY DAYS SERVICE STATION: 1 MILE.**

The Samsung starts ringing again.

Cursing under my breath, I reject the call and turn the blasted thing off, tossing it alongside its mobile sibling on the passenger seat. I don't want to speak to Harriett. I don't want to speak to that vile *bitch* ever again. This is all *her* fault. If she hadn't been pestering me, then I would have had full concentration on the road. And just what the fuck does she want? She's had her pound of meat (pardon the expression) off me for this month. And I hope she enjoyed it, too; she won't be getting anything else.

Rivulets of rain stream down the windscreen as a thought pops into my head. I look at the two mobile phones riding shotgun. Maybe I should ring the police. I don't have to give them my name or any details. I don't have to tell them anything specific. After all, I don't want to get involved. Perhaps I should ring them *anonymously*, and tell them that I *think* that I *might* have seen a car hit *something* on the M6 junction. It'll probably just turn out to be a traffic cone, but I should ring them all the same, right? I should do that. It's my duty as a motorist, after all. *Better to be safe than sorry*, that's what Darcy says. Trouble is; I won't be able to use either of the mobile phones. Cops will be able to trace the call.

Not that it matters, anyway. By now, I am *certain* that it wasn't a person that fluttered in front of my headlights. And before I can give the thought anymore reflection, a car draws level with my speeding Honda in the next lane, beeping its horn.

Oh, God, please don't say that somebody was behind me on the service ramp. Did they see what I did? Did they see me hit that woman? No, there was *no* woman. I didn't hit *anybody*! It was just a trick of the lightning. Or maybe a wild animal - most likely a fox - dashing across the road. Whatever it was, it was certainly **NOT** human. I mean, what kind of a lunatic goes hiking through the woody area at the side of a motorway late at night, anyway? I've done nothing wrong.

Slowing down, I squint through the murky driver's side window at the car roaring down the next lane – a white Toyota Prius. Barely, I can make out the blurred features of an old woman hunched over the steering wheel, staring directly at me. This unsettles me tremendously, making my teeth itch. Why is she looking at me? She's not honking her horn anymore or trying to get my attention. She's just *staring*… and I don't mean at the road, either.

Jesus, this relic hasn't taken her eyes off me once. Is she fucking nuts? You're on the motorway, love, for Christ sake! Look at the fucking road! Daft old codger will cause a pileup! Fingernails on one hand sink into the hard leather of the steering wheel as I gesture frantically at the road in front of me – in front of *us* – with my other. It does no good, though. The senile old bat just goes on gazing at me with wide and unblinking eyes.

"What the hell are you doing?" I roar, my breath stonewalling against the glass, misting it up. "You're going to *kill* yourself!"

Lightning engulfs the black sky. Thunder grumbles like an upset stomach.

I am just about to scream another pointless warning to the old woman, when the most bizarre thing that I have ever witnessed in my life occurs. The old fossil – still plummeting down the slippery M6 at seventy miles an hour without watching where she is going – peels bloodless lips back over yellow dentures and *sneers* at me.

Now, I don't mean she smiles. Nor does she give me the type of *you've been caught, you little scamp* warning grin that my Gran used to give me should she catch me with my hand in the biscuit tin. No, this batty old woman with wispy white hair and not a day under eighty, *sneers*, revealing a dental palate feathered with greenery; as though she has been drinking tea straight from the bag.

Then she flips me off with her middle finger.

It's the most bizarre thing that I have ever seen in my life. Dumbfounded, I watch her scrunch her wrinkled face into a mask of hatred and snap her

21

head back and forth against the headrest, cackling manically, thumping the wheel.

With my heart pounding in my ears, guilt throbbing in my chest, I turn back to my windscreen just in time to find it filled with the humungous arse of an Eddie Stobart trailer. The snout of my bonnet is just inches from the racing truck and I can clearly read both the registration number and the **HOW'S MY DRIVING?** sticker above twinkling taillights.

"Fuck!" I scream high-pitched.

Instinctively, I stomp the brakes and swerve the wheel, but the road is too wet for the rubber to bite and find purchase. I end up skidding towards the goliath, pulling obsessively on the steering wheel, surprised when the Honda doesn't flip out of my control and go barrelling into the next lane – taking that crazy sod out with it.

Knees lock. Arms cramp from wrestling with the steering wheel. Voice grows raw and gnarled from screaming.

This is it, I tell myself, bracing for collision. *It's all over. At least it will be quick. Would have been nice to have got a chance to hold my daughter for the first time, though, or tell Darcy how much I love her. Would have been nice to tell Harriett Bronte just where to stick her fucking job.*

Then, for the second time tonight, the front wheels of my Honda hit the soaking wet tarmac of a service ramp. Miraculously, I narrowly avoid hurtling into one of Mr. Stobart's cherished trucks and go on my merry way towards the Happy Days service station instead.

Thank God for that. I could murder a Latte.

CHAPTER 3

Pulling over in the empty car park of the Happy Days service station, I idle my engine and take a couple of seconds to gather my scattered thoughts; listening to the soothing rain and trying to work out just what was going on. I cannot make any sense of it. Why did that old woman try to make me crash into that truck? Did she do it on purpose? I don't wish to believe such a thing, but she *must* have. My hands are trembling uncontrollably, and I cannot stabilise my breathing. My heart is throbbing much too fast for comfort, feeling as if it has been thumbed inside of an iron horseshoe.

Nothing about tonight makes much sense. Why did Harriett call? She's never done that after one of our illicit rendezvous. Usually we have our time together in the hotel… and that's it; wham-bam-thank you-ma'am. We never ring each other on the spur of the moment. She might send the occasional flirty text or snap of herself, but that's usually during the run-up to one of our 'appointments'.

Harriett approached me with her indecent proposal after we shared a drunken kiss behind the photocopier at the office Christmas party. Cliché, I know, but from the very start of our lustful agreement, Harriett made the rules – *her* rules – very clear. *She* would decide when and where we were to meet once a month. I was *not* to contact her under any circumstances, as this was most certainly *not* an affair. She loved her husband wholeheartedly, but his recent bout of chemo had left him impotent and he had become unable to fulfil his marital obligations. I was merely a stopgap; providing Harriett with a service that her husband could no longer provide. And for this, I would receive a measly fee to help pay for the arrival of my baby girl – which speaks volumes about how much of a disgusting man I truly am.

Then there was that *thing* that I *may* or may *not* have hit on the service ramp. Combine this sudden thunderstorm with how eerily abandoned the motorway is - not forgetting that geriatric looney - and you could describe tonight as being the biggest clusterfuck of my life.

I park the Honda as close to the service station as I can get to avoid getting soaked on the run from car to station. A huge duck pond is to my left and, to my right, a small hotel stands back from the station. It must be one of the chain's only lodgings that Harriett and myself have yet to taint.

Apart from my Honda, there's only one other vehicle parked on the gravel of the car park, a saturated Ford Focus at the far end of the grounds. Erecting the lapels of my jacket, I grab my iPhone, slide it into my pocket, leaving the Samsung - and *Harriett* - behind, and open the door. Climbing out, I step straight into a puddle. Dirty rainwater fills my shoe, and I hiss a curse, grimacing as the icy coldness soaks through my sock. Thumbing the fob,

I lock my Honda and dash for the main entrance of the service station, squinting through driving rain as it plasters my hair to my skull.

Concrete steps lead to automatic doors. Bright fluorescents reveal two vending machines standing sentinel-like in the foyer – one dispensing hot drinks, the other crammed with enough chocolate, crisps, and peanuts to make Jamie Oliver bust his gut. Grabbing the iron railing running the length of the steps, I ascend two at a time, desperate to be out of the storm.

A young man is exiting the station food court as I barge into the foyer. Shaking rain from my jacket, I pull my phone out to ring Darcy. I don't intend on telling her about the incident on the service ramp or the crazy woman trying to make me crash into the back of that truck. I don't want to worry her. Besides, causing stress in her condition is only going to add to my woes. I've got enough shit to be dealing with right now. I should ring and let her know that I am going to be home later than expected. Not contacting her at all could cause the same problems that I am eager to avoid.

I step to one side to allow the young man wearing the expensive-looking suit to pass. Speed dialling Darcy, I press the phone to my ear, but don't notice the man stopping abruptly at my side. Dropping his laptop bag to the ground, it lands with a cringing *crack*. Darcy's phone rings once and then she answers it.

Before I can speak, the young man swings a clenched fist into my jaw, sending me sprawling backwards into the automatic doors. Landing on my back in the foyer, I instinctively roll onto my side, staggering drunkenly on hands and knees as the young businessman strides across to inflict further damage.

"Wait... what..." I mumble, clutching my aching jaw. Forcing myself to my feet, I stagger confusedly through the sliding doors, back into the station. "What are you doing?" I demand to know. "What the hell's your problem?" Spittle peppers the air, flecked with blood from where my teeth have gouged my tongue to Swiss cheese.

The man turns around without a word, crouching to pick up his laptop bag, harnessing the strap over his shoulder. Breathing heavily, he marches across the foyer towards me. I back up against the wall, balling my shaking hands into tightly clenched fists, preparing to defend myself against this moronic idiot.

"Is there a problem here, sir?"

I spin on my heels to see the largest security guard that I have ever seen in my life step out of a door in a corridor leading – according to the sign above his head – to the gents' toilets. He's wearing navy trousers with a matching sweater over a light blue shirt. He hooks his brisket-sized hands to the leather belt strapped around his waist. Rubber soles of his black boots squeal against the glimmering floor tiles. Clearing his throat unnecessarily, the security guard crosses arms that *could* belong to a professional wrestler over a chest that *could* belong to a professional bodybuilder.

"This… this… *idiot*… just hit me for no reason!" I bluster at the guard.

"What are you talking about, sir?" the security guard sighs, shaking his colossal head.

"What am *I* talking about?" I chuckle, humourlessly. "What the hell d'you *think* I'm talking about? I'm talking about this tosser—"

The words clog curtly in my mouth as I realise I am pointing an accusing finger at the empty foyer. There's nobody there. Son of a bitch must have had it away on his toes as soon as the security guard showed up. Even took his laptop bag with him. Feeling foolish, I try to explain my quandary to the security guard.

"Sir, I think you should have a cup of coffee and take a break from the road." The guard bends at the hip to pick up the scattered pieces of my phone, offering the screen, case, and battery to me in separate hands.

"What?" I frown, accepting the *Meccano* set. "Did you not *see* him?"

"Only thing I saw was you on CCTV flying backwards into the doors. Caught yourself a good one on the head, did you? You should take a seat in the restaurant for a couple of minutes."

"So, you're telling me you didn't see the man?"

"What man?"

"*The* man!"

"Sir, you need to calm down."

Now it's my turn to sigh. "So, you didn't see anybody else?"

The security guard shakes his huge head, reminding me of a rabid St. Bernard.

"He was *here!*" I hiss, pointing to the very ground between the guard and myself. "Clear as sodding daylight! What's wrong with you, man? Are you blind? How could you have *not* seen him?"

"Sir, I think you need to calm down and call somebody - a friend or a relative. You've taken a nasty bang to the head. Do you have a wife or a

31

partner that I could ring? I think that phone of yours has seen better days."

"I don't need you to call *anybody* for me!" I finger the blood trickling from my mouth, dribbling down my chin. "See that?" I hold up bloodied fingertips. "I suppose you're going to tell me I am not bleeding, too."

The security guard furrows his thick uni-brow. "Of course, you're bleeding, sir. Not surprised really, seeing how hard you hit the ground. I can get you a glass of water to swill you mouth, if you'd like. The toilets are just down that corri—"

"I don't *need* you to get me a glass of water! I *need* you to tell me that you saw the man who punched me – punched me full force in the face!"

"Sorry, sir," the guard mutters solemnly. "I didn't see anybody."

My throat feels as though it has restricted to the size of a pinhead. Palms are clammy and, when I try to swallow, the coppery fluid coating my tongue makes me retch. Tastes like I have a mouthful of two pence coins.

"You... just... didn't..." The words refuse to form coherently in my mouth. I look over the beefy security guard's shoulder - into the food court - and see how barren of life it is. Apart from a young blonde woman crying hysterically into a scrunched tissue, it is emptier than Joey Essex's skull. I turn my attention back to the guard. "Did you really not see the man who punched me?"

The security guard sighs as though I have just asked him to lend me twenty pounds. He removes his baseball cap by the peak, running a gorilla-sized paw over his shaved head before slapping it back on. "Look, sir, for the last time, I watched you on the camera come into the service station alone. I watched you throw yourself backwards - alone. Thought you might have slipped on the tiles; what with the rain being so bad tonight."

"And you're *certain* that you didn't see another man?"

The guard shakes his head solemnly. "No, sir. There was nobody else with you."

Nodding, I back off through the sliding doors, stomping into the downpour, hurriedly descending the concrete steps leading to the car park. Risking a glance over my shoulder, the stocky guard slowly waves goodbye. It's all I can do to stop myself from sprinting for my car.

CHAPTER 4

Phone's fucked.

Don't know why I'm surprised. Seems to be the night for shit-poor luck. The screen of my iPhone is shattered, and it won't turn on. I pulled onto the hard shoulder shortly after leaving the service station – and it's dopey fucking 'security guard' - and tried fixing the phone, but it was no use. It is dead.

I am now back on the M6 again, gushing through the night, still struggling to get my head around how strangely deserted the motorway is. I've seen a couple of headlights whooshing towards me from the opposite lane and, occasionally, a lone car will hurtle past on this side of the carriageway. But the motorway is nowhere near as congested as it usually is. No doubt the late hour and furious storm will be responsible to a certain degree but, after tonight and everything that's transpired, I would be more than naive to blame *only* them – I would be fucking *stupid*.

I thought about using the Samsung to ring Darcy. It's still on the passenger's seat but, despite how much I am craving to hear her voice, I cannot bring myself to switch it on. The phone represents everything that I am – cheap, shoddy, easily bought.

Managing to find a bottle of water in the glovebox, I used it to rinse my mouth at the roadside. Still cannot believe that arsehole hit me. I didn't do anything to offend him or provoke an attack. Hell, I wasn't even *looking* at him. Caught me with a strong blow beneath the chin, though. Nearly knocked my jaw down to my arse.

Another signpost looms in the distance, illuminated by headlights, silhouetted by shrubbery. Drawing nearer, I am slightly alarmed to realise that it's advertising *another* Happy Days service station to be one mile away. I swallow hard, hearing something click in my throat. Could it be the *same*

Happy Days that I have just left? The one where I was assaulted and ridiculed.

No, it *can't* be.

For starters, it would be navigationally *impossible* to backtrack and return to my original location without taking any side roads or reversing. I have been driving straight down the motorway ever since leaving that forsaken place. And I've not taken any back roads, which could spin me around.

So, it's a different station then, right? A chain company like *Little Chef* or *Subway*. Of course, it is. I bet the motorway is crammed with Happy Days service stations all the way from Birmingham to Manchester. I suppose that makes a little more sense than my Bermuda Triangle theory. Smiling at how stupefied my overworked brain can sometimes become, I ease down harder on the accelerator, steering the motor through the raging downpour towards the second service station.

My nerves are still shot-to-shit, and I can't rid my mouth of that sour taste of stale blood. Also, my bladder is close to bursting. If I don't pull over soon and relieve myself, then I am going to combust. Need a strong coffee to regain my composure, a payphone to call Darcy, and a couple of paracetamol for my pounding head. And it looks like I am not the only one in need of a drink. The dial on my fuel gauge is inching closer and closer into the red. If I am going to avoid chugging home on fumes, I will need to fill the tank up. And, apparently, there's only one place that I can do that: The Happy Days service station.

Twinkling lights further ahead.

Frowning, I slow down as my headlamps reveal the backend of a Ford Focus parked zigzagged on the hard shoulder.

What the hell has happened here? I ask myself. *Has there been an accident? God, I hope not. Wouldn't be surprised, though. The roads are lethal tonight.*

Looks like some idiot was going too fast and had to stop suddenly, skidding into the metal barrier bordering the roadside. Drawing level with the car, I notice oily smoke spewing from the bonnet. The driver's door is open and…

Oh, God, no!

A body is sprawled over the wheel.

Plumes of black acrid smoke broil from the crumpled engine, clouding together, blocking my view of the lane as they swirl in front of the windscreen. I indicate to nobody that I am pulling onto the hard shoulder and manoeuvre the Honda across two empty lanes, bringing it to a stop just ahead of the smoke-spewing Ford. Without thinking, I climb into the rain and run towards the crashed car, splashing through puddles, craning my neck around the open door of the Ford.

The woman's dead. I have *no* doubt in my mind about *that*.

Wide, accusing, bloodshot eyes stare directly at me from a twisted and smashed face. Blood dribbles like runny yolk from between the woman's parted lips; nostrils, ears, eyes… *everywhere!* I can see several lacerations carved across her forehead. Her nose is crooked, disjointed, obviously broken along the bridge. The flesh around her eyes has turned ruddy, tinged with deep purple welts.

A car surges past. It's on the other side of the carriageway, and I barely notice it at all. Despite knowing that she has already gone, I place two fingers to the side of her neck, searching for a pulse. Not finding one, I remove my hand, realising that my fingers are tacky with blood. Quickly rubbing my hands against my saturated coat, I back away from the car and, not knowing what to do, close my eyes, dropping to my knees; forehead kissing the cold concrete of the hard shoulder.

Thunder roars rabidly above.

When I open my eyes again, I realise that I am looking at a mobile phone resting in her lap... along with her two front teeth. I can only assume that she was accepting or making a call when the car spun out of control and hurtled her face-first into the steering panel.

There's something about the waterfall of blonde hair - stained red with geysers of blood and pink globs - gushing over her ruptured face that strikes a chord of recognition inside of me. I don't know how, but the young woman looks vaguely familiar. I am quite certain that I don't *know* her, but I have *seen* her before; like a stranger you might nod to daily, never learning their name.

But how? And where from?

I swallow a rush of vomit, forcing myself back to my feet. And then it dawns in my mortified brain just who she is.

It's the blonde woman I saw in the last service station - back when I was arguing with the security guard. She was in the food court, crying. Shit, I saw her alive no less than ten minutes before she crashed! How the hell has she managed to get in front of me? Granted, a few cars *did* race by, so there's every chance that she *did* leave the station and overtake me, but I have been driving the whole time with the pedal pressed against the floor.

Surely, she would have had trouble *catching up*, never mind *taking over*.

What the fuck is wrong with me? Why am I just standing here like a spare part, getting pissed wet through, gawking at a dead blonde girl? Do something *productive*! Call the police! Call an ambulance! Call the fucking *Ghostbuster's*! Call *somebody*!

But then I remember I *can't*. My phone is in three different segments back inside the Honda.

Never mind, you've got the Samsung. Use that. Turn it on, call for help. While you're at it, ring Darcy, too. Some secrets are too big for even you *to hide.*

I back away from the busted Ford with my hands interlocked at the back of my head. I am just about to sprint back to my car when my eyes fall upon the phone in the young woman's lap. Snatching it from her crotch, I thumb the nine button three times, raising the phone to my ear, anxiously waiting for the emergency services to answer.

Exactly *who* answers my call for help, I don't think I will ever know – or want to find out. But the quivery voice that sniffles and sobs into my ear does *not* sound like any call operator I have ever spoken to before. In fact, they do *not* sound like a *man* or a *woman*, but more *childlike*. At first, I struggle to hear what they are saying. All I can focus on is the grumbling thunder and rushing rain. But then I catch more sniffling, more weeping, and it becomes clear that the 'operator' is *crying*. With my index finger poked inside of my left ear, the dead woman's Nokia pressed to my right, I mutter a "Hello?" into the mouthpiece.

What I hear turns my blood to slushy ice.

Through a hoarse voice, grown phlegmy with crying, I hear a child's voice whisper "Is he still there? I don't want to come out if he's still there."

Frowning, I ask who I am talking to.

"Never mind, sir. It's not important. He's already taken my skin."

"What? Who are you?"

More crying. More sobbing. Hysterical this time, threatening to perforate my eardrum.

Shocked, wringing wet, shivering, shit scared; I open my mouth to say *something* when the child voice beats me to the finish line.

"He peeled me alive, sir."

"Who are you talking about?"

The call cuts out.

Droplets of rain splotch against the blank screen as I lower the phone from my ear and stare, slack-jawed, at it.

What the fuck was *that*? I mean, what the *fuck* was *that*? *Who* was it? A kid? It certainly sounded like one. But what would a child be doing in an emergency service operations room? What did they mean 'he has already taken my skin?' Who has? What's going on? And what was that bollocks about being peeled alive?

My heart shivers, flinches, and my whole body breaks out in gooseflesh. *Somebody's just walked over my grave*, that's what my mother used to say about the feeling. Those words have never sounded so ominous before.

Breathing laboriously, bile sloshing about in my gut, I toss the dead Nokia back into the equally dead woman's lap, and run back to my Honda. Skidding to a stop, I jerk open the door, hop behind the wheel, scoop up the Samsung off the passenger seat and turn it on. Whilst waiting for the digital logo to upload, I twist the key in the ignition and rev the engine. Checking both lanes are empty – of course, they are – I shoot straight back onto the motorway.

Once the phone has warmed up, I start dialling Darcy's number when it beeps twice in my hand. Gasping loudly, I nearly drop the phone into the footwell again, a wave of deja'vu washing over me. Running a hand through my soaking wet hair, I glance from the ravine that I am ploughing through, to the screen of the phone, and see a little envelope with the words **1 MESSAGE RECEIVED**. It has *got* to be Harriett. She's the only one who has this number.

Sparkling lights dazzle through the inky blackness to my left. I'm approaching the service ramp that will lead me to the second Happy Days. Although, concerns about relieving myself or sinking a hot coffee could not be further from my mind. I still need to contact the police about the dead woman. And when I do, they are going to want to speak with me in person. How dodgy is it going to look if I just drive straight past the first service station that I come upon after discovering a dead body? After all, the blonde woman and I were in the previous Happy Days *together*. I remember seeing her upset. And we must have left around about the same time. If some ruthless detective was to come here and speak with that plonker of a security guard about how peculiar I was 'supposedly' acting, then they might put two and two together and come up with ten. Christ, before I knew it, I could end up facing a whole barrage of awkward questions.

And I *am* almost out of petrol.

I should pull over and call the police from the next service station, call Darcy, too; explain everything to both - and I do mean *everything*. That *thing* on the service ramp; the old woman flipping me off and trying to make me crash; the young businessman man who hit me in the service station; the dead woman who died in the collision; the weird kid (which *must* have been a crossed line) and what they said about people being dead. I need to confess *all* – and yes, that includes the reason I was out at such a late hour on a stormy night in the first place – Harriett Bronte.

I drop the Samsung and its unread text back onto the passenger seat and swerve across the carriageway without bothering to check for oncoming traffic.

Gliding up the service ramp, screeching to a halt in the gravelled car park of the Happy Days station,

I stare through the rain-splotched windscreen with a flutter of unease tingling inside of my stomach, and a dead woman's blood staining my hands.

CHAPTER 5

I pull over next to the fuel island, wheels of the Honda locking, wet tyres grinding loose gravel into tiny mounds. Shoving the door open, I spring out into the raging downpour and unlock the fuel cap. I have spent quite a bit of time in the torrential rain tonight, so much so that I am now soaking wet; even down to my underwear. After tonight's done and dusted, I will be surprised if I don't catch pneumonia.

Waving to get the attendant's attention, I feed the nozzle of the pump into the car, squeezing the lever until petrol flows. Once I have a full tank, I replace the fuel pump, dashing across to the garage to pay.

Because the hour is so late, they won't let me inside of the garage for security reasons. Instead, I must pay via the reinforced glass serving-hatch.

When I ask the young Arab behind the counter if there's a payphone on site, I receive a churlish shrug, followed by something in a foreign language. However, I follow his pointing finger in the direction of the service station and, thanking him nonetheless, I collect my debit card and jog across to the station with a taste of iron broiling at the back of my throat.

I've always thought it odd as to why roadside restaurants all look the same. Call into one of the many *Burger King* or *McDonald's* dotted about the country, and you will find each one to be a carbon copy of the last, including the seating layout. And it would appear to be the same story with the Happy Days service stations, too. Despite being located a good few miles south to its sibling, this station is *identical* to the previous. It's uncanny how mirror-like the two stations are. I can't imagine how much precise attention and intense planning the construction crew must have invested to get the Happy Days to all appear the same – even down to the large duck pond on the opposite side of the car park.

As I climb the concrete steps leading to the main foyer, should I expect to find two vending machines dispensing chocolate, crisps, and hot drinks standing at attention like custodian watchmen on either side of the sliding doors?

What do you reckon?

Wiping my feet on the coir mat, I step into the entrance and glance from left to right at the rows of shuttered *Tie Rack*, *Costa Coffee*, *W.H. Smith's*, and *Krispy Kreme* stores. Were there shops in the first Happy Days? I can't remember. To be fair, I barely got through the front door before that scumbag punched me. I think there *might* have been shops, but I don't know for certain. A salad bar hums annoyingly to my right, boasting a display of white, brown, and seeded bread rolls above refrigerated pots of shredded lettuce, chopped tomato, diced cucumber, and squeezy bottles of condiments.

Nobody's in the main foyer, so I pause to catch my breath and regather my thoughts. I think there is an invisible anvil crushing my chest. At least that's what if feels like, and, try as I might, I cannot reduce the clambering beat of my heart. Nauseous, I walk like a man wearing lead stilts towards the food court, passing a row of arcade machines with flashing screens and fake machine guns.

Is the food court situated at the back of the station, like in the previous Happy Days? Well, yes, yes, of course it is. Why should I expect any difference? I grab the acrylic handle of the door as my ears pick up the stifled yet distinct beat of hip-hop music blasting from behind the closed partition.

Inching the door open, I peep around the jamb. Gobsmacked, I take in the raucous crowd and, pushing the door further ajar, I slip like a hand inside of a glove into the food court – into the *melee* – my brain refusing to believe what my eyes are seeing.

Scantily clad women wearing figure-hugging outfits portraying nurses, schoolgirls, French maids, and cheerleaders are dancing provocatively on top of two tables. Applauding the seductive gyrating, a group of businessmen sit around the table, stuffing twenty-pound notes into the women's garters, puffing on cigars. A teenage girl with brunette hair wearing nothing but a red bra and thong is sprawled across another table; legs wide open, positioning herself into the best angle to show off her heaving implants.

At the back of the room - where the food would normally be on display - a ginormous black man wearing a leather trench coat and headphones is spinning the decks of a turntable, nodding his head back and forth in time to the music; dreadlocks dancing like Medusa snakes. Artificial smoke spews from a funnel above the DJ, masking the crowd.

A commotion separates the horde in the middle of the court as two businessmen – both looking like they could make serious money by modelling for

Ralph Lauren – clatter across the food court, punching, kicking, and scratching the shit out of each other. One of the men lands a vicious right hook, knocking the other guy to the ground. He doesn't get up. The crowd advance over his body like an incoming tide.

What the hell is going on? Who are these people? Where have they come from? What are they doing? And who the fuck gave them permission to do it in a service station?

There is a screen hanging from the ceiling broadcasting a fetish porn movie. Swaying on numb legs, head spinning, stomach churning, bowels bubbling, I watch a naked woman on the plasma screen groaning soundlessly as she masturbates on a dirty mattress. Chained to the foot of the bed – shaved bald, painted red – a mistreated chimpanzee is sniffing the air, relentlessly trying to free itself so it can pounce on top of the squirming woman.

In the corner of the food court, an elderly man with a broken-veined nose and white hair is sitting on a chair. Wearing a black gown (which is streaked around the crotch with silvery stains), the unmistakable collar of a priest is noosed around his scrawny neck. One hand cradles a bottle of Jack Daniels, the other keeps the tangled locks of a young blonde woman's head in his lap. The girl must be no older than sixteen.

Desperate to flee the horrendous freak show, I turn around, accidentally knocking a child's highchair over. The chair disintegrates into a thousand gnarled pieces against the tiled floor, and I go sprawling over the wooden limbs. Barely keeping upright, I grab the shoulder of a nearby young man to steady myself, twirling him around.

It's the son of a bitch who hit me in the other Happy Days!

Thunder roars with frustration overhead, rattling the very foundations of the station.

Dripping wet, I step forward, tiny puddles forming on the floor beneath me. Split-second later,

I lose my nerve, backtracking two paces. "*You…*" I gasp through a wheeze. "*You…*"

This isn't *real!*

It *can't* be!

Not only is the clean-cut bastard amongst the mass of the food court, but that bullshitting security guard is, too. Confused, I look around the heaving crowd, spotting that screeching hen party – including the inebriated woman who flashed me her arse – in the ocean of humanity.

None of this is real, I tell myself. *It can't be. You're dreaming, Brucey, baby, that's all. Time to wake up… wake the fuck up!*

That wrinkly old woman who gave me her middle finger on the motorway shuffles from behind two naked men who are rubbing mustard and mayonnaise into each other's hairy chests. Hobbling awkwardly on arthritic legs, hunched at the hip, gasping for breath, she is wearing a long anorak over fleeced boots and has a plastic rain hood tied beneath her jowly chin. Terrified, I watch her sniff the air like a famished animal, then potter across to the shrieking hen party.

That's it. I've seen enough. I'm leaving. I refuse to waste another second surrounded by such *filth* and *depravity*. Whatever's happening at the Happy Days station has *nothing* to do with me. I am getting into my car and I'm not stopping – no matter what – until I get back home.

Psyching myself up to gallop for my car, one of the young women dancing on the table (dressed like an air stewardess) hitches her short skirt up to her waist, and the drunken crowd cheers. Her lace underwear is spattered with something which *might* be – but *isn't* – dark red paint. Shoving my way through the chaotic noise, I hear the woman scream, "Look everybody, I've just come on!"

Her revolting words causes my heart to shudder, making me believe I must have nodded off at the wheel and woke up in the bowels of Hell. I've never seen or heard anything sicker or deranged in my life… and I doubt I ever will. That is, of course, until the dancing women help the old woman onto the table and, slipping a rummaging hand into her floral skirt, she removes two glistening fingers and holds them up for the observing crowd. Looking directly at me, she shouts, "Look everybody, so have I!"

Sinking my teeth into the knuckles of my clenched fist is all I can do to stop the vomit from rushing up my throat. Walking slowly - but purposely - through the main foyer, I step into the pouring rain. Head hung low, shoulders hunched against the roaring wind, I unlock my car and climb back behind the wheel. Revving the engine, I drive back onto the motorway.

As soon as the second Happy Days service station slips out of my rear-view mirror, I slap on the brakes and bring the Honda to a screeching halt, kicking open the door and vomiting all over the wet road.

CHAPTER 6

I'm going home. I am not wasting another nanosecond driving up and down this motorway – going from one horrific service station to the next - in the pouring rain. My head is aching. Every time I blink, it feels like I'm wearing contact lenses made of razor wire. I should be looking after Darcy; I should be showering Harriett off my body; I should be looking after my pregnant fiancée, not running away from sordid orgies. I don't have a clue what was happening in the Happy Days service station and, to be truthful, I don't *want* to know. I am out of there now, and that's all that matters. I don't intend on pulling over again until I reach my front door.

I still can't get that dead woman out of my head. And why *does* she look so recognisable? It feels as if I *know* her. But that's ridiculous. I only laid my eyes on her tonight. Sooner or later, I will have to contact the police about her death. What do I tell them? Do I mention all the crazy shit that's happened tonight? Will they believe me? Will Darcy? Or will they think I am just doolally and sign me over to the nearest nuthouse? Do *I* believe what I saw at that second service station?

Look everybody, I've just come on!

It *was* real. It *had* to be. I didn't imagine it. Nor *could* I even if I wanted to.

Look everybody, so have I!

And I heard *that* with my own ears.

The Samsung beeps on the passenger seat again, alerting me to another text message. Glancing from the empty road, I pick the phone up and read the message. It's from an unknown number. Reading the text, my eyes narrow and my face creases as I study the words on the screen.

WHO R U?

Swallowing hard, I scroll to the next message, which has been sent by the same number. Without knowing I am doing so, I ease my foot down on the accelerator. Finding the second text, I open it, despite my brain advising me to throw the phone out the car window.

MY NAME IS CASTOR BRONTE. I FOUND UR NUMBER ON MY WIFE'S PHONE. ALONG WITH THIS...

A blurry photo of Harriett Bronte fills the screen, followed by a message:

Hey, handsome, the bed is nice and comfy☺ Cum over... me. X

Of course, I recognise the picture. It's the calling card Harriett sent from the hotel this afternoon, back when I was still at the office. She must have forgotten to delete it. Fuck! Shit! It's her *husband!* I'm talking to Harriett's *husband!*

The mobile vibrates in my hand again as another text comes through. With my fast-beating heart hammering against my ribcage, I press accept and read the next message.

CARE TO XPLAIN?

Flash of lightning. Belch of thunder.

Then the phone starts ringing.

Startled, I drop the Samsung as the unknown number appears on the screen. The phone ricochets off the gearstick for the second time tonight, tumbling into the footwell, landing next to the accelerator

"Shit," I hiss as the phone continues to ring.

Ducking my head beneath the wheel, my free hand searches frantically for the phone as the other continues to steer. Teeth clench together as groping fingers find the Samsung, grabbing it as though it is eternal youth. Propelling myself back behind the wheel, I shake my head to clear the black floaters in front of my eyes. Heart beating fast; blood pulsating in my ears; breathing shaky; mouth parched. When my vision clears completely, I have just enough time to see the blonde woman illuminated by my high beams before the front of my bonnet smashes into her, flinging her into the shrubbery of the roadside.

Instinctively, I stomp on the brake pedal, pulling the handbrake at the same time, bringing the Honda to a slithering halt, almost spinning completely out of control. Pushing the door open, I clamber out into the rain, which has suddenly turned into nothing more than a light drizzle. The woman is sprawled on the wet road of the motorway – only we are no longer *on* the motorway; we are on one of the service ramps, which lead to the carriageway. Brooding clouds are a lot lighter… but it looks as though a storm *is* brewing.

Leaving the Honda gurgling in the middle of the lane, I race across to the woman - legs stretching, arms pumping to gain momentum – and throw myself to my knees - to her *mercy* - snaking one hand beneath her cracked skull, holding her cold hand with the other, squeezing gently.

"Don't die," I plead, stroking the side of the woman's face. "Please don't die. Not again."

Reaching into my jacket, I retrieve my phone – my *functioning* iPhone, not the Samsung – and call an ambulance. Thankfully, this time, an emergency operator answers the call - not a crying child babbling about dead people. The operator takes my details and informs me that men and women wearing green coveralls with the word **PARAMEDIC** emblazoned across their backs are currently putting down mugs of steaming coffee and climbing into white vehicles with flashing lights and screaming sirens.

I kiss the blonde woman on her forehead and promise her that everything is going to be okay, trying my hardest to keep her awake. I know who she is now… and not just because I saw her corpse little less than twenty minutes beforehand. Finally, I know what tonight was about. It all makes sense to me.

The scream of approaching sirens filters through the evening air.

She's the bottle-blonde with more curves than the Monte Carlo racetrack who serves pints of watery lager down at the Golden Wings. The girl I had a one-night stand with. The girl I cheated on Darcy - the mother of my unborn daughter – with.

The drunken mistake. The walk of shame. The girl I treated appallingly and with about as much respect and dignity as I have probably shown every other relationship and meaningless one-night stand I have ever gotten with. What was she doing out here beside the motorway? Why was she out in such Godawful weather?

It's not important. None of it matters anymore.

Pulling my jacket from my body, I blanket the young woman with it, kissing the back of her hand, apologising, crying, begging forgiveness, asking her to stay with me. Wrapping her bleeding body up in my arms, I pull her closer and, together, we listen to the distant thunder rolling closer and closer.

***

END OF THE LINE

A Novelette

James Jobling

CHAPTER 1

I love the city at night. The sights are raw, humanity stripped down to the very core. Sights, sounds, smells—all magically disgusting. I have just spent the last nine hours sitting in a stiflingly hot conference room, listening to Natasha, my moronic supervisor, whittle on and on about 'customer care' and 'commissioned target audiences'. The whole thing bored me out of my bleeding skull. Loves the sound of her own voice, does that one. Stupid bitch! But the whole dreadful day is over - now I have two days to get steamed and gallivant. After all, isn't that what they invented weekends for?

It's only a ten minute walk from the office to the train station, but I have at least twenty minutes to kill before my train departs, so I decide to stroll along the crowded streets at a leisurely pace, savouring the strange sights and spicy aromas. It's eight o'clock on a Friday night, and the promenade is just as packed as I had expected it to be. Revellers from both hen and stag parties flock to my coastal hometown most weekends to pound booze, sniff drugs, shag meaninglessly, and gorge on junk food; swapping the scenery but not the *habits* that the grime-and-crime city offers. The atmosphere tonight is erratic. The air is a vile cocktail of aftershave and beer and chip fat and raunchiness. I can hear the tide coming in from my left, but a huge billboard announcing the dates for a stand-up comedy show featuring a once-funny comedian has blocked the sight of the sea. Squawking seagulls hover above. A group of middle-aged women wearing too-much makeup and too-short denim skirts, complete with pink cowgirl hats, stagger past me. They are all wearing T-shirts with the words LINDA'S BIG SEND OFF emblazoned across droopy breasts. If ever there was a walking advertisement for Broken Britain it was these screeching delinquents; all spray tan and Primark knee-length boots. They are massacring a Whitney Houston song as they stumble along, laughing, singing, glugging from a passed around litre of Smirnoff Ice. One of the women bends over the ocean wall, vomiting, spilling her stomach contents onto the shingle below. She grants the world and his wife an unwanted view of what lurks beneath that stonewashed miniskirt. A couple of famished seagulls drop onto the beach and begin snipping their beaks through the regurgitated slop. My stomach contracts further when I catch a glance of a purple thong imbedded amongst mounds of blotchy pink flesh. I put my head down and cross the road.

The Match of the Day ringtone on my iPhone begins bleating and I sigh inwardly. I already know who the caller is without having to look at the screen. I bloody knew this was going to happen. I told her it would. In fact, if memory serves, it had been Nadine's idea to invoke the 'no strings attached' clause at the end of our date the other night. I had been firm with her. I had been upfront. I had admitted that I was only interested in a little fun. Nothing serious. Truth be told, I don't usually go for women who are older than me, but Nadine looks great for a forty year old, and those tits are *incredible*! It was Nadine who had invited me back to her flat for some 'no strings attached' *indulgencies*. It had all been her idea, yet what happens come Monday morning? Ring-ring-fucking-ring!

I ignore the call and leave it for voicemail to pick up (again), flashing my ticket at the bored-looking attendant sitting behind a glass screen. He barely even looks up from his computer monitor. I walk onto the platform and breathe a sigh of relief when I see how empty it is. Aside from a broad, muscular guy with a gnarly beard and bright red Mohawk and a group of chavs fucking around near the hot drinks dispenser, the platform is eerily abandoned. Usually at this time on a Friday evening, it's crawling with agitated suits, eager to get back home for a scotch on the rocks. But tonight there is a weird calmness to the stillness—like it's just *meant* to be this way. I flop down on a steel bench and allow my head to loll against the cold headrest.

A cracking sound emanates from the circle of youths and they quickly move suspiciously away, one of the little bastards cockily eyeballing me. I hold his stare until he passes and only then do I glance down at the drizzle-speckled ground.

It's resentful knobheads like these who are stomping the great out of Great Britain. They group together outside of kebab shops or on parks; smoking joints, terrorising the older residents of the neighbourhood, the whole time flipping the middle finger obnoxiously into the face of their ancestors and the law. The worst part is the vast number in which they breed. There was a little social disorder here a few years ago, back when that poor black kid was shot in London by the police. These youths really rallied together then and totally outnumbered the cops. Bloody morons!

A whoosh of warm air followed by an amplified roar announces the imminent arrival of my train. A second later, it gushes from the black tunnel, like a gigantic earthworm made of metal. I stand up and wait for the doors to slide open.

CHAPTER 2

I scramble aboard and grab an empty window seat. The freedom that the platform had promised is quickly mocked and ridiculed once I board the train and it feels like all of these commuters have liaised with each other behind my back to meet up at a different stop and board the train there, luring me into a false sense of security. Silly, I know, but the train is swamped with people. Straightaway, the usual sounds wash over me—a baby crying, a mobile phone ringing, coughing, a crisp packet being rustled open—and then the nauseating stench of stale grease and fried onions waft in front of my nostrils as somebody further down the carriage digs into a Big Mac. We're all crammed like sardines in here. I shudder inwardly when the obese man sitting beside me fumigates his nose with a loud sneeze;

nose-spittle peppering the back of my hand. Shit, if even one of these passengers has a contagious disease, it would spread like a fucking bushfire in here. Isn't that how all epidemics are spread? This ginormous man beside me could be returning from Africa for all I know. He could be an Ebola carrier. He could *have* Ebola! I can feel my heart drumming against my ribcage now. My phone begins ringing again – *da-da-derr-da-derr-da-da-da* - I can feel it in my pocket, vibrating against my thigh. Luckily, the garble of conversation spewing through the carriage is drowning out the rattle. I close my eyes and pray the majority of commuters will be getting off at the next stop in Berrywood.

"Erik? Erik Millstein? Is that you?"

I snap open my eyes at the sound of my name and my stomach growls irritably when I see who has chosen to sit next to me. Spencer Rogers!

I have just spent nine hours listening to the congested breathing of this overweight slob! Nine fucking hours inhaling that disgusting meat and potato pie stench of B.O. wafting from the foul bastard. Spencer-fucking-Rogers! The moron who sits opposite me and Stanley in the office; the clown who still lives at home with his parents despite being in his late forties; the dirty bastard who pops pimples in the canteen, regardless of whether anyone is eating in there or not; the oaf with yellow collars, silvery cuffs. The smelly bastard whose rancid breath stinks as though he has been gargling with vinegar instead of mouthwash. He's here now! Here on *my* fucking train!

Sod this for a game of soldiers! I've had to spend all day breathing in his toxic filth. I cannot bear to spend another second in his slobbery. I smile politely and lean forward.

"Hey, Spence, I didn't know you lived in Marshfield."

The instructor blows his whistle from outside. Every second counts now.

"Marshfield? No, that's not this train."

"Is it not?" Even *I'm* shocked by how genuine my tone sounds. Should have taken a career in acting instead of working for the council.

"No, you big douchebag. The next stop on here is Berrywood." He smiles creepily, revealing yellow teeth that look like rows of Sugar Puffs. He leans forward, his huge girth swallowing his thighs. "Shit, you dork, you'd best get off before we take off."

"Yeah, you're right." I stand up and manoeuvre around the huge breathing-pandemic sitting next to me. He sneezes once more as I pass, blasting my crotch with his germs. I grimace and feign a worried frown. "I'll see you Monday morning, Spencer."

"See you, mate."

Mate? Is he serious? I push my way into the aisle and hurry towards the next carriage, rushing as though I am desperate to relieve myself. Tripping over an unseen suitcase viciously poking from under a chair, I just manage to scope another empty seat in front of me. It's one of those foldable chairs that you sometimes see solo passengers sitting on, or flustered fathers lumbered down with the pram and bags, whilst the missus and kids sit in comfort. It's usually this poor soul that everyone expects to press the door release button when the train finally docks, too, as though being scrunched between the revolting toilet and snack-cart isn't bad enough, they now expect him to be a team leader!

I *"excuse me"* and *"can I just get past there, mate"* my way to the draughty, swaying carriage-connection and flop the empty seat down. The train has pulled away from the station already, but I hope everyone leaves me in peace for the remainder of the journey now. That daft cunt believed me when I said I had gotten on the wrong train (and there's no reason for him not to—he believes we are *mates* for Christ sake) and from this position, in-between two carriages, he can't see me. In fact, I can barely make out the sealed doors entombing him. Smiling at my own cunningness, it takes a couple of seconds to realise a young Chinese woman is smiling back at me.

She sits on one of the chairs facing me but I missed her on my break-neck gallop for the empty chair. Don't know how though – she's a *stunner*! Her hair is as black as the Arab desert at midnight. It falls around her wonderfully smooth-looking face, just reaching her shoulders. Her teeth look as though they have been bleached—no, scrap that, they look *painted*—white, and her eyes...oh those *eyes*...

And that's when it dawns on me that I am still looking at this Chinese woman and I am still *smiling*. I must look like a creep; one of those weirdo's that children make up urban legends about; who live alone; who the neighbourhood kids dare each other to ring the doorbell and run away every Halloween night. One of life's oddballs who looks like he could—and probably *would*—squeeze the last gasp of breathe from a child's throat. Or a Chinese woman's.

Stop fucking grinning!

The train is really picking up speed, galloping past a row of disused warehouses, hurtling towards the canal bridge. We will soon blast by the cinema and bowling alley on the complex centre before hitting the industrial estate where the Curry's and PC Worlds are stored. I glance away from the window that takes up much of the door in front of me, and once again, my eyes lock on the Chinese woman. She is *still* smiling.

"Tickets, sir."

The young conductor distracts me from my reverie and I tap down my coat and trousers, searching for the tickets I know I purchased, but struggling to locate their whereabouts. Thankfully, I find them in the breast pocket of my coat just as the conductor begins eyeing me suspiciously. The train judders unexpectedly to the right and I almost stagger into him. He scribbles something on my ticket, clips it, hands it back, before continuing down the carriage. I slip the ticket back into my pocket and look up to see that Chinese woman has moved seats. During my brief distraction with the conductor, she has managed to swap her window seat on the right, for an aisle seat on the left. What the hell? How did I not see her move? She's about four rows in front of me now, still watching, still smiling.

The bright spotlights of the complex centre ignite the car park stretching below. I can see a dozen or so souped-up cars razzing up and down, racing one another. They are the local petrol-heads who converge on the car park at the back of DFS every Friday evening to show off their jazzy motors and talk carburettors. Yes, they can be loud—boisterous even—but they are not exactly *dangerous*. This doesn't stop the council from paying two police officers to stand at the centre's entrance whenever the Cruisers (as they like to call themselves) show up each week. It's quite ridiculous really. There's no point in it whatsoever. They are just kids idolising a lifestyle they don't *have* and would never *want*. Rap songs blare out of their car CD players and they say to themselves "yeah, I could have a bit of that…so long as I'm not late home for tea!" I have never once heard of them getting into trouble or starting fights. In fact, the council would probably be better off hiring those two police constables to patrol the train station on a Friday evening. Maybe they'd be able to slap an injunction on those little arseholes vandalising that drinks dispenser earlier.

I look back up. Now that Chinese girl has moved closer, I can see her in finer detail. She is wearing a white knee-length dress with red roses decorating the front, and sandals strapped to her feet. There's a Chinese symbol tattooed on the side of her hand, which she lays atop her faded denim jacket on her lap. She is still smiling at me and I'm really starting to feel taken aback now. She's a pleasure to look at—a right pair of legs, the kind you could imagine wrapped around your neck—but the fact that she hasn't took her eyes off me is a little unsettling. Perhaps I should acknowledge her somehow. Maybe give a little nod. Then it dawns on me that I may have offended her. Could it be that? Is that why she has been eyeballing me for so long? Have I offended her somehow? Surely not! And even if I have, wouldn't she be scowling instead of smiling? Perhaps it's some kind of a feminist protest. They've certainly chose the right 'victim' to revolt against. I look up and stare her straight in the eye. The Chinese chick doesn't even blink.

Blackness snatches my view of the city like a poltergeist snatching a rattle from a baby. I am left looking into the dark eyes of my own reflection. Ears do that uncomfortable thing which happens every time the train sweeps through a tunnel, leaving me to feign a yawn so they will pop. I loll my head against the wall and close my eyes. There is a stale taste of iron carpeting my tongue. My mind immediately goes on safari, aimlessly pondering what tonight should bring.

It has been a long day. A few beers and a kebab in front of the TV sounds appealing, but then again, I am thirty-four, not *forty*-four. Nadine is definitely up for it, too. Soon, I'm going to have to start thinking about settling down. I'm not talking kids here (not straightaway anyhow) but I am well aware that my better days are reaching their expiry date. I ache far longer than I used to after five-aside football nowadays, and although I'm not officially labelling it a 'beer-belly' just yet, I am aware of the podgy kangaroo pouch pushing against my belt. Nobody wants to die alone. Everybody wants to meet 'the one', whether they admit it or not. Those people who say they don't are just bitter recluses who have bitten from the fruit of love only to enjoy the taste so much that they dare never to take a second bite. Maybe I should give Nadine a chance. I suppose the age gap between us isn't that wide. Like I said earlier—those tits *are* incredible!

The train begins slowing down. We must be pulling in to Berrywood. One more stop after that and I'm home. I blink my eyes open and decide to give Nadine a text—

-oh shit-

That Chinese woman has moved from her seat again, but this time she's in the *same* fucking connection as myself! What the hell does she want? She's just standing behind me—still *watching*, still *smiling*—and it's only her faint reflection in the window, which reveals her at all. I didn't hear her enter; didn't hear the whoosh of the automatic doors opening; didn't hear the click-clack of heels rebounding off the metal floor. I heard *nothing*. But here she is. I swallow and hear something click in my throat.

The train rushes out of the tunnel and dusk fills the carriage once more. The platform for Berrywood begins speeding alongside the train. Clusters of commuters begin dragging themselves wearily from their seats, stretching cramped bodies, pulling down luggage from the overhead storage shelves. I spin around to see that Chinese lady, but find only a swamp of passengers, all eager to get off the train. Looks like my wish for the majority of commuters to get off at Berrywood is going to come true. I scan the faces of the people behind me, but I cannot see that Chinese woman. Was she following me? *Is* she following me? The screen of humanity all around reveals nothing but flushed faces, suits, and suitcases; a kaleidoscope of people all focused on that one door—and the guy standing in front of it—m*e*!

I keep looking for the woman, but it's like trying to find a needle in a pile of needles. If she's still in here then she must be at the back of the crowd, squished in the corner.

The train lurches to a complete stop but there is still that annoying delay waiting for the automatic doors to unlock. There are about fifteen people standing behind me and around about the same number waiting *on* the platform, reminding me of two bloodthirsty Viking tribes facing off on the battlefield, eager to allow the fighting to commence.

85

The door release button flashes green and I fist it, quickly stepping back before the stampeding crowd crush me to death. The doors part, and the tide of humanity surges. A wayward elbow accidently pokes me in the stomach. I grunt more with surprise than pain and look through the open doors at the wet platform illuminated by the spotlights overhead.

That's when I see her.

Standing at the back of the platform, away from the train, away from the crowd, a woman is patiently waiting…a Chinese woman…a Chinese woman wearing a white dress dotted with red roses…a *smiling* Chinese woman wearing a white dress dotted with red roses! Could this indeed be the very *same* Chinese woman that I saw on the train no more than twenty seconds ago? Surely not! It would be *impossible* for her to have departed the train without me having seen her. The constrictive crowd in front of me are wedging their way through. She couldn't have slipped past. No way! But that *is* her!

It's impossible, I know, but there's no doubt in my mind that it's the *same* person!

The wheels of some dozy mare's suitcase rolls over my toe and I have to chew on my tongue to stop myself from reprimanding her. An announcement bellows from outside, muffled in here due to the hushed conversations and footfalls echoing throughout the carriage. I look over to where she's standing—where she is *smiling*—and now there is no doubt in my mind that it is the same person. How she managed to get by without me noticing her, I don't know. But that's the same woman from the train. It's *got* to be!

Unless it's her twin. Yeah, maybe that's it. I bet one of them lives over here in England and the other one—the one still submerged beneath human rubble—lives over in China. She has simply flown over here to visit. Of course, that's it! Their mother probably used to dress them in identical clothes as children and they've kept the habit going into adulthood as a mark of respect to their mother's wishes. I bet they even make long distance phone calls every day just to see what the other one is wearing! 'Ah, hi, I just phone to see what colour bra you wear.'

Ha, barmy sods…

…you're rambling. You're *nervously* rambling.

Before I can convince myself that I'm just being overly paranoid, and it's nothing more than coincidence that the Chinese woman on the platform looks identical to the Chinese woman on the train—weight and height included—a sharp pain engulfs my big toe. The blonde in front of me has stepped accidentally on the very same part of the very same foot that the silly cow with the suitcase abused no more than five second ago. And she must have been wearing stilettos due to how precise and excruciating the pain is. I wince and embed fingernails into my fleshy palm, but before I can try to slither any further away, the tide of humanity catches me like a twig in a fast-flowing river. It pushes me towards the open doors. I struggle and shove against the horde, but it's no good. There are too many.

As the crowd herds me through the doors of the train, someone roughly pushes me onto the wet platform, where I stumble over my own feet and land in a crumpled heap on my backside.

CHAPTER 3

When I was a teenager, barely old enough to shave, barely old enough to buy a legal pint, I went to a rock concert with my brother, Owen, at the town hall. At some point during the gig we got separated amongst the cheering crowd, but I can still clearly remember to this day calling his name, reaching for him, standing there looking like a plumb in the middle of the heaving ocean of dancing, gyrating rock fans as my brother slipped further and further from sight. Eventually, I relented and rode the wave to the back of the hall where I spent the remainder of the concert, standing in front of the gents' toilets, barely able to see the stage, with a foul stench of disinfectant scorching the back of my throat. That's how it feels now—minus the eye-watering stench! I try to battle my way back on the train, but to no success. They barged me through the open door and left me sprawled on the platform. Selfish twats! Too concerned with their own pitiful, self-centred existences. I climb back to my feet and brush droplets of rain from my coat, grains of dirt from my trousers. The crowd have headed towards the escalator leading into the main station, so I take a second to compose myself before heading back towards-

-the train farts steam and takes off.

"Hey!" I bellow, chasing after the locomotive and slapping the window. "Hey, I need to get back on!"

The train just keeps going through; gathering speed, really going for it.

This is bloody absurd! The staff here is incompetently comical! My feet barely touched the platform before the train started moving again. Isn't there some kind of ritual between pulling into stations and departing? Isn't some Fat Controller meant to blow a whistle to let the driver know no more passengers are trying to get off or on? Am I not at least granted the prerogative of realising I'm on the wrong station and hopping back on the train without getting blindsided like this? It's not a massive problem, I know. More of an inconvenience than anything else. It's not exactly *late*-late. I don't have to be anywhere. It could be much worse. I know I'm taking this to heart, blaming the staff when I know full well it had been the commuters who had forced me off the train, but it's been a bitch of a day—a bitch of a *week*—and all I wish to do is to fold up in front of the TV with a cold beer and a hot curry. Now I have to prance about finding out when the next train is due to-

-she's *still* there!

The mob on the platform have finally fanned out, making their way into the heart of Berrywood station, leaving only myself, the train conductor (smoking a crafty cigarette whilst pacing back and forth) and that moronic Chinese woman from the train. She is standing beside a vending machine and looking straight at me. She is smiling as though she knows the hilarious punch line to some clandestine joke that only she has the privilege of knowing. I've had enough of this shit! I don't care if she's intellectually disabled or if she has some kind of condition—this is all *her* fault! I'm absolutely furious! If she hadn't been playing silly games on the train, switching seats, then I wouldn't be in this predicament now! And there is no doubt in my mind that she is the same bird as the one I saw in the carriage because there is only *one*—not *two*—lurking behind that there vending machine. I don't have a clue how she managed to sneak past and to be honest, I don't really care. These childish pranks need to stop! She's about to get the length of my tongue whether she likes it or not!

"Oi, I want a bloody word with you!"

The Chinese woman carries on smiling.

The conductor spins on his heel, the butt of the cigarette wedged between two pale lips. "Can I help you, sir?"

"Nah, mate, not you," I stop halfway between the edge of the platform and the dispensing machine. "Her! I want a word with *her*!" I point my finger at my very own Chinese Katie Hopkins.

The conductor peeps over his shoulder and cocks an eyebrow before taking another inhale from the rollup. "You're aware there's nobody there, right?"

What? Is he blind as well as stupid? I look back at the Chinese woman still standing beside the vending machine, clear as day, and she raises one hand, wiggling her fingers. A wave! She's fucking *waving* at me!

"There," I gasp. Even I'm shocked at how siphoned my voice sounds. "She's right *there*!"

The conductor turns around and follows my trembling finger towards the dispenser—towards the loony—and he smirks before placing the death-stick back between his lips. "Of course she is." There's no denying the sarcasm saturating his tone.

Fingers clutch tightly around the conductor's arm. I can feel the rough material of his damp overcoat; catch a hint of Old Spice. I look into his battleship-grey eyes and realise how psychotic I must look. Quickly, I let go of his arm and step back, struggling to reclaim control of my rabid breathing.

"I'm sorry. It's just been a long day and this crazy woman," I nod towards the vending machine, "she's been stalking me!"

"Stalking, you say?"

"Yes. I got pushed off the train at this stop and—"

"Pushed off, you say?"

I know when somebody is taking the piss out of me. There is no emotion on this bloke's face, no sympathy in his tone. He's laughing at me behind those slate-coloured eyes. The fingers on his cigarette-free hand smooth down the corners of his handlebar moustache. When he speaks again, I am astonished at how sour his breath is. It is so bad I can only assume his wife looks forward to his farts.

"Look, mate, I know—"

He waves me silent. "Do you have someone who look's after you?"

"What? Are you taking the piss?"

The conductor smirks and picks a rogue piece of tobacco from between his teeth. Shaking his head, he spits onto the train track. "Get out of here, son."

"Will you just look?"

"I think your little joke is over. On your way, sir."

"Please, just look—"

"I don't need to *look*. There's no sod there."

"You really *don't* see her?"

"Only thing I can see is some moron who is three very short seconds away from getting one of these."

He holds up one hell of a meaty fist as though it is Exhibit A and grabs a handful of my shirt and tie. "I don't want to hear any more of your shit, you hear? I've already had enough of your bollocks, *mate*. Now be a good little fruitcake and have it away on your toes before I really lose my patience."

He releases me and shoves me back a few paces. I step right back, anger pumping through my system. My fingers curl into tight fists. The conductor doesn't flinch. Billowing smoke cascades down my throat. I hold a cough captive and instead turn on my heel, walking away from the conductor, brushing his greasy handprints from me. I step on the empty escalator, aware of only *one* set of eyes watching me. As I pass the vending machine, I'm shocked to discover the Chinese woman has gone. Just vanished into thin air. Is that it? Has she had her little bit of 'fun' at my expense and gone back to crawl under her rock?

Grabbing the rubber handrail, I realise that I have jumped the gun on this assumption. I look up to the top of the escalator and see a Chinese woman wearing a white dress dotted with red roses with a pair of sandals strapped to her feet standing at the top, watching my slow ascend. The bony tentacles of a panic attack enclose around my throat. The escalator reaches the top and I step off. I am now only a mere inch from her, but I cannot bring myself to *look* at her. I cannot bring myself to *speak* to her. I do not have a clue what is going on, but right here, right now, my gut instinct is screaming for me not make any form of contact with her. I have never had to depend on my survival flair before, but now it's *all* I've got. I move away from the escalator and into the heart of the station, aware that every breath I take, every move I make, she'll be watching me.

CHAPTER 4

The Black Sun.

Christ, what a shithole. Not even Keith Richards would glug a beer here.

I had followed the crowd from the platform through the station and onto the entrance where an empty taxi rank and bus stop exposed themselves to me. That Chinese woman had, of course, followed me; always no more than a few footfalls behind. My plan had been to lure her into the open and try to lose her amongst the masses. Either that or find a copper on the beat and report her. Unfortunately, I didn't get the chance to do either.

Instead, the craziest thing I have ever seen in my life came about. And those alarm bells in my head transformed into an air raid siren wail. You see, once I stepped out of Berrywood station, that same very throng of commuters that had pushed me from the train—that I had personally witnessed leaving the station—evaporated. I don't know *how* nor do I know *where* they went. I just know that one minute they were there—eager to jump into the back of a cab or pick up their vehicle from the car park across the road—and the next they were gone.

Poof!

Drizzle had turned into rain. Rain had turned into a tropical downpour. It drilled so hard against the top of my head that it stung. The heavens, it seemed, had dilated and gone into full-blown labour. I hadn't wasted too much time out in the torrential cloudburst and instead sought shelter in the doorway of a shuttered HMV. There I had pulled out my mobile and rang Owen to come and pick me up. It went straight to voicemail so I tried my best mate, Brad, but his phone just rang out. He had probably taken that dolly from the chemist out. So much for just a casual thing, eh? Lying bastard!

Flustered and more than a little soggy, it was then that I clapped my eyes on the pub across the main road, the Black Sun. It didn't look much from the outside, but it was, quite literally, a port in a storm. It had a roof, it'd be warm and best of all it'd be dry. I could relax with a beer and keep an eye on the rank for the next available taxi. It was either that or stay here and freeze my bollocks off with You Know Who.

As if on cue, the creeping silhouette of a small woman had stepped out of the station and into the pouring rain. And I knew straightaway *who* it was. So I had set off like a greyhound, bolting right across the main road, not even checking for traffic. The roads were as abandoned as you'd expect to find them at 6 a.m. on a Bank Holiday Monday. Light from the overhead lamps reflected in the puddles. It didn't particularly strike me as 'weird' finding the roads so vacant. I had never visited Berrywood before (and certainly never intended to again) so for all I knew this was the norm. Perhaps after eight o'clock at night, this place locked up its doors, closed its windows, and said good night to the world. Although I must admit, I was surprised to see no taxis parked at the rank or any buses at the stop. Saying that though, that large crowd *did* disperse at a mysteriously rapid pace. Maybe it wasn't so *mysterious* after all. I didn't really give a shit. I needed to get away from that Chinese whore! I needed to lose her!

With that thought in my head, I had passed a closing McDonald's and charged into the Black Sun.

"What can I get you, mucker?"

I turn towards the barman and order a pint of lager before dropping onto a bar stool, sighing a breath of relief.

"You look troubled, mister." Weak-looking lager trickles into a pint jar. Beady eyes dissect me from beneath wire-framed glasses held together by gaffe tape on the corner hinge, reminding me of Jack Duckworth. "Everything okay, like?"

"Not really." I place a crumpled five-pound note on the bar. The barman slides my beer over and snatches the money away as though he's convinced I'm an unscrupulous character playing a cruel trick on him. He waddles over to the antique-looking till on the opposite side of the bar, pings open the drawer, and waddles back with my change. He pushes the stacked coinage towards me.

"Haven't seen you in here before," the barman grunts, scratching his baldhead. Years have faded the blue tattoos that covered the backs of his hands. Doves, love hearts, meaningless squiggles, and every lags favoured Love and Hate decorate his knuckles. He had even inked his fingers. Chunky gold bracelets decorate both of his thick wrists. When he growls something resembling a smile, I can see the gold has also made its way into his dental work. I take a hefty swallow of beer and wipe a frothy moustache away with the back of my hand.

"You look a little flustered."

"It's been a mad day."

"Aye? Somebody after you?"

"Something like that."

"Not the old Bill, I hope."

"What? No, no, nothing like *that*."

"Welcome to the Black Sun then."

This place maybe a dosshouse but I have to admit the beer tastes fucking *marvellous*! I knock back the whole pint in three giant swallows.

"You look like you needed that," the barman tells me, grinning, revealing more golden bridgework. "Can I get you another?"

"I'm not sure that I should."

"Then you're not sure that you *shouldn't*."

The Black Sun reminds me of the seedy Labour Club that my old man used to drink in before he had his stroke. The carpet beneath my stool was probably a lush red once, but due to decades or muddy work boots, spilled drinks, inebriated scuffles, vomit, and wear-and-tear it's been reduced to a faded dull flesh-pink that not even a famished cannibal would find appealing. I spot islands of its original colour in an ocean of grime and the dreaded purple welts of spilled wine. Walls are woodchip, whitewashed, turned yolk-yellow at the top thanks to nicotine ash clouds. Framed pictures of dogs playing snooker or poker. Net-curtains looking like they are about to fall down. I think the last time they had seen a washing machine, the Luftwaffe had been paying these parts a visit.

"Get me a refill," I demand.

The barman chuckles triumphantly and nods his bulbous head. "'Ard day at the office?"

"You wouldn't believe me if I told you."

"Ah, women trouble, eh?" He pours my lager and places it in front of me.

I sip more gingerly this time. "Something like that."

The door opens and slams closed. I almost jump out of my skin, expecting to see that Chinese schizophrenic in the doorway, then relax as two old timers shuffle towards one of the empty tables, anoraks drenched with rain. Shit, I bet these two even *remember* the Luftwaffe! Aside from myself, the barman, and the two newcomers, there is only one more punter perched in front of the bar, nursing a tumbler of whiskey. He's a burly behemoth with cropped hair and a trimmed goatee, and he's wearing one hell of an expensive-looking leather jacket. He has more gold on his fingers than Mr. T wears around his neck. I can't stop myself from thinking how uncanny the resemblance is between this huge oaf and that lout who won the lottery all those years ago who squandered the lot on booze, coke, and hookers. Wait…did I say *squandered*?

"So let me guess; the wife's cooking's that dreadful, you'd rather come here and socialise with society's deadbeats rather than face *another* burnt mac-cheese?"

The barman reaches under the bar and removes a glass tumbler. He pours a generous measure of whiskey and slides it down to the mean-looking grunt at the end of the bar who catches it in one huge paw without looking up. The whole remarkable episode reminds me of the cowboys I once idolised from the Saturday morning westerns. The ones I used to watch with Mum as a boy.

I gulp my beer and stifle a belch. "No, no, I've just had a very strange—"

She's *there*!

Not inside the pub. No, she's too shrewd for that. Instead, that Chinese wench is standing outside in the pouring rain, looking in through the huge bay window overlooking the bar. There is no filthy curtain obscuring the view here. Her hands are at the side of her face to block out any intruding shadows and she is squinting into the pub. I know straight away she is looking at me. Even though she is nothing more than a silhouetted shell, I *know* it is her. There is no doubt in my mind. I can feel it in my stomach; knotting my innards together. My hands start shaking again. What little bravado I gained by downing the ale, is already contemplating coming back up. What the hell does she *want* from me?

I jump off the stool with the intention of finding out once and for all, but instead of landing on the vile carpet, I end up crashing into the brute from the end of the bar. He staggers backwards as I accidently drive the point of my elbow into his right moob. The Neanderthal grunts through his nostrils and drops both his phone and drink onto the floor, the phone clattering loudly against the bar. Whiskey inflicts another scar on the ghastly carpet and I wince as I see an iPhone obliterate into a million different segments on the floor. The barman runs both of his tattooed hands over his head. The two geriatrics don't even look up from their game of dominos.

"You silly, daft cunt!"

I grimace as though I am a timid rabbit in a Richard Adams novel, and press myself up against the bar. Opening my mouth to say sorry, it occurs to me that I have already apologised at least a dozen times. I stop rambling and offer to buy him another drink.

"Is that going to fix my fucking phone, you prick?"

Spittle peppers my face. I grimace as particles sweep past my parted teeth and set up camp on my tongue. Before I can do anything about it though, a handful of my shirt—and myself—are hauled into this ugly bastard's twisted face. His cheeks have blustered to a fierce red.

"I'll pay for your phone! I'll pay for it!"

"You're damn fucking right you'll pay for it!"

"Ah, come off it, Smithy," the barman sighs, lifting the hatch of the bar and stomping onto foreign ground. "Can't you see it was an accident, man?"

"Stay out of this, Joe," the maniac warns. "This is between me and this fucker here!"

"Look, mate, I'm sorry about your phone. Really, I am. I've had this crazy Chinese—"

My lungs deflate fully as a huge fist sails into my sternum. It feels as though this moronic fool possesses the strength to obliterate my ribcage, grab my fast-throbbing heart, and crush it in one gigantic hand if he wanted to. I didn't even know I was flat on my back until he's picking me up again, hauling me headfirst into the bar. Teeth clamp down on my tongue. My mouth fills with blood.

"Smithy, that's enough!" I hear the barman holler. And then my ears pick up something else. I don't know where that banging is coming from, but it's close, very close, right behind-

-then it doesn't matter at all as a size 10 Timberland boot kicks me full-force in the middle of my back. The blow evicts all air from my body. Winded, bleeding, I crawl away on hands and knees, desperate to get away from this savage psychopath. All fears revolving around anything remotely Chinese or wearing white dresses dotted with red roses dissolve from my pain-racked mind.

All I can do is try and make a run for the front doors.

I find my feet, but all this does is put me in direct line for another punch—right on the button this time—and again I'm on my back; blood trickling from both nostrils. Pain is pounding inside of my head, feeling as though I have endured root canal with no anaesthetic.

The banging has gotten louder. Very loud. I look up and see that the barman is bundling that rabid menace into the lavatories. Thank God for that! The two elderly geezers have not even looked up from their game of dominos throughout the whole ruckus. Either they are afraid of getting involved or they are used to 'Smithy's' outbursts by now. I mean, they *do* look like regulars.

Breathless, I roll onto my back and close my eyes. I can hear the rain pouring against the thatched roof of the pub. I can hear thunder growling in the distance, but above that, I can hear Smithy and the barman shouting at one another in the toilet. The door keeps opening a few inches before slamming closed again. I can only assume the barman—Joe?—is blocking Smithy's path.

The banging has morphed into an industrious hammering now. And it's coming from the window—the Chinese woman! I look across and even though all I can see is an insidious hellhound lurking beneath the murky cover of a stormy night, I can see tiny fists beating the glass. Bloody Nora, she's hitting the glass with her fists! If she keeps it up it'll go through! The two old geezers don't seem to hear her? They must be deaf or hard of hearing or something. Then the jukebox fires up on its own accord…and my heart really starts to foxtrot.

Frank Sinatra starts crooning about love and marriage going together like a horse and carriage in the silky way that only Ole Blue Eyes can, but I swear neither of the old lads' have moved. It certainly wasn't my new best mate, Smithy, or the barman who have put the song on. They are still going for it hammer and tongues in the toilet. The juke could be on automatic play, I suppose. They do that at the Lamb and Gate; one minute you're tucking into your ploughman's and the next 2-Pac is blasting through the speakers, scaring the crap out of you. Yes, that's most probably it.

The banging against the window abruptly stops. A strange *tink* flows throughout the pub, and then silence follows. For the first time since entering, the two golden oldies playing dominos turn around, watery eyes looking at the huge crack running straight down the middle of the bay window.

"Shit," I whisper to nobody in particular. "She did *that*."

For a couple of seconds, all I can hear is Sinatra serenading the pouring rain. Then one of the old men surprises me by speaking.

"You okay, son?"

I nod my head slowly. Eyes glued to that cracked window.

"There should be some paper towel behind the bar," the other old dinosaur claims. "Go help yourself. Joey won't mind."

I lift the hatch and step behind the bar. There is indeed a roll of blue towel (used for cleaning down the tables and bar, I suppose) so I snatch off a length and hold it beneath my nose. "That guy's a lunatic!" My voice is muffled due to the towel absorbing bloody mucus in front of my mouth.

"Smithy? Oh no, he's okay, really. Just a tough nut, you know?"

"No shit," I replace the crumpled paper towel with a fresh strip and realise the gush of blood is beginning to stem. Looks much worse than it actually is. I should be grateful, but I'm not.

"Oh yes," the old man sitting nearest to me confides. He either didn't pick up on the sarcasm in my voice or he has chosen to ignore it completely. His eyes are wet. Tears trickle down his broken-veined cheeks, but he's not crying. Blocked tear duct, you see? My Nan suffered with the same. He

114

is wearing a flat-cap and a wax overcoat. A wooden walking cane leans against his chair. "He's a…oh, what is he again, Keith?"

"A gangster," the presumed 'Keith' answers.

"Ah, yes, a gangster. That's what he is. Old Keith here and myself used to knock about with young Smithy's granddaddy back in the day, didn't we?"

"Aye, sure did. He was a bloodthirsty gobshite, too. Mixed plenty with old Duncan Dwain back in my boxing heyday." He delivers two punchy jabs to thin air.

"Did you hell. You silly sod. He cleaned your clock every time you stepped into the ring with him, if memory serves correctly."

"Then you must have some shrapnel lodged in your canister, you stupid bastard. And keep running your lips, Jake, and you'll be getting some of what this fairy here just received."

He holds up an arthritic clump of a claw. Both men chuckle mischievously. I feel like I'm watching a Laurel and Hardy sketch. Stupid old codgers!

To hell with this! I march from behind the bar and make for the exit.

"Watch how you go, lad," Keith sniggers. His white-haired drinking companion sneers at me from behind his half of mild.

"Are you two staying here?" I shake my head, wishing this crazy dream would just end.

"Don't see why not," Jake says through a toothless smile. "There's a fiver on this game."

"Big stakes," Keith adds.

"Last of the big spenders," Jake said.

"But that guy is a thug!" I spit. "He's just kicked the hell out of me!"

"You'll be doing a lot less sinning then, won't you?"

Both men chuckle cheekily.

I shake my head and turn back towards the door. I can still hear Smithy and Joey cursing at one another. Joey is shouting something about 'not losing my license again!'

I turn towards the two old farts. "I'm going to call the police, you know? I'm pressing charges against him."

"Do as you must," Keith smirks.

"Will you do us a favour, though?" Jake asks.

"What's that, old timer?" I sigh.

Both of the old fossils look suspiciously towards the cracked window. Jake's voice loses all trace of humour. "Take *her* with you."

I pull open the door and run out into the pouring rain.

CHAPTER 5

Once I leave the Black Sun, I rummage inside my coat for my phone so I can call the police. Part of me is begging to leave it, just grab a taxi and go home. It's been a crazy night thus far and the thought of spending the next few hours in a police station makes my head throb. Everybody knows how laughable the police are. Even if they did arrest Smithy, the only thing he would receive is a caution. And that would only be if I were extremely lucky! Now, it's his word against mine. I can't see the barman or those old fogies coming forward as witnesses. All he has to do is deny ever having laid eyes on me, and then what? I'll have a rabid fucking drug-dealer looking for me, that's what!

But on the flip side of the coin, he *did* assault me. I know my nose has stopped bleeding and aside from the gash in my tongue caused by my own damn teeth, I'm okay. But why should I let him get away with it? I need to make a stand. I need to make him see that I am not prepared to let him get away with beating people like that.

And whilst these thoughts are surging through my mind, it dawns on me that I don't even *have* my phone. It isn't in my coat. It isn't in my trousers. It's not in my inside breast pocket where I sometimes keep it to avoid it getting wet during rainy spells. In short—I don't have it! It must have fallen out of my pocket. It's probably somewhere inside the pub. For God's sake!

I contemplate going back for it. It's most likely somewhere near the bar. It won't take more than a few seconds to find it. Probably fell free when that arsehole was chucking me about. I can't leave it there. Not with him. All of my personal numbers and email addresses are in it (not to mention a couple of saucy snaps of Nadine), but he'll also have access to my social network accounts. Who knows what that sick bastard would post on Facebook or Twitter!

Going back in there is suicide. It was only the sheer intervention of luck that saved my skin last time. Going back inside now would be more than just waving a red flag at a bull—I'd might as well be holding up its offspring's decapitated head! No, best make it back home and call the customer helpline; get the phone blocked ASAFP! The taxi rank is still empty so I'll have to call one…but without a phone…

I run around the corner, the soles of my shoes skidding on the rain-slicked pavement, prompting me to grab the drainpipe at the side of the pub to avoid going arse-over-tit into the road. Not that it'd matter much. I cannot believe how quiet this place is. I have only been here in Berrywood for ten minutes and I haven't seen *any* traffic. Not even on the fucking main road! In fact, the only set of headlights I saw incinerating the mist was when I had first left the station, and even they were heading *out* of town. I try to swallow but my mouth can't produce saliva. The back of my throat is sticky, hands shaking, breathing raspy. Where is she? Where the hell *is* she?

Rows of detached houses face me across the road. Slated rooftops made slippery from the pouring rain stretch around smoking chimneys. They're your usual two-up two-down council set-up. Nothing major. Just wood, mortar, and brick separating five separate families from living as one. The kind of properties that the council build quickly on the cheap and then struggle to understand why they are always wading through a backlog of callouts. In one of the upstairs windows, I can see a little boy sitting cross-legged on the sill. He must be around five years old. He's looking down at me and smiling. I can feel genuine warmth radiating from that innocent smile. Not like that crazy fucking Chinese bitch! This is a *real* smile! No grinning! No sneering! No leering! The boy wiggles his fingers at

121

me and I realise he is waving. I give him a little salute back before running off down the street.

A belch of thunder. The rain has matted my hair to my skull so I put my nut down and continue charging through the deluge; heart pumping acidic blood and electrifying my sprinting legs. I splash my way towards the main road and once again, the sight of the barren lanes clogs the breath in my throat. At half-past eight on a Friday night these six lanes—three on either side—should be bumper-to-bumper with cars and buses. What the hell is going on? I can see an all-night café on the same side as myself, just a few yards away. Surely, somebody there will be able to help me, even if it is just the loan of a phone. The smell of burnt bacon and grilled grease sizzles from an air ventilator in the brickwork, incensing the rain. I put my head down against the downpour and jog towards the café.

CHAPTER 6

Sliding a hand through the beaded fly-screen, I push it aside and step into the café. It's a grubby place. A real greasy spoon. The kind of place where they serve sweet tea in chipped mugs and clusters of hardened ketchup or mustard always seem to pepper the red and white chequered tablecloths. Every precinct or high street has at least one of these fleapits. Nowadays they are easy to spot a mile away—they are the ones with no hygiene-rating certificate in the window.

Like the Black Sun, there are customers in here, but unlike the Black Sun, they are not *all* men. There's a burly man wearing a lumberjack shirt and a baseball cap. He sat behind one of the tables closest to the doorway, and was tucking into an all-day breakfast, which really *did* look like it had been there all day! A male cyclist is standing in front of the thumb-smeared glass counter waiting to place an order. Well-endowed men should *never* go out in public wearing spandex shorts. As the harshness of the bright fluorescents overhead diminishes, I can hear the type of screeching and squawking that only mourning seagulls should be capable of creating. I turn to my right and see that same fucking pissed hen party that I saw back in Spindale. Jesus, where did they come from? They are still wearing those lung-squeezing T-shirts that make them look like they have been *poured* into the garments. They are passing a bottle of wine around, singing at the top of their voices. Shit, some poor cunt's going to be *marrying* one of them!

I approach the enamel worktop with its billowing tea urn and currant buns wrapped in cellophane, and I make eye contact with the greasy Italian frying chips in a deep-fat fryer. He smiles at me before wiping his hands on his dirty apron. The

Insect-O-Cutor crackles as it claims the life of a curious fly. I step in front of the counter.

"Yes, fellah, what can I get you?" His accent is more Danny Dyer than Italian Stallion. I tell him I need a payphone.

"You don't want anything to eat? Nothing to drink?" There's a frown of disdain etched on his olive-coloured face.

"No, I'm fine, thanks."

"Fine?"

"Just the phone."

"Through there." He says. An overgrown thumbnail crooks towards a closed door with the words TOILETS AND BABY FEEDING written in marker pen on the wood. The words remind me of an angry child's scrawl.

"Through there?"

"The payphone is in there."

I thank the chef and leave him to shake the dripping fat from the grate of chips before slopping them on a plate. I push open the side door, which leads into an alcove. In front of me are three closed doors. Drawn in the same marker pen on the door to my right is a matchstick man with the words GENTS written above. On the door in the middle is the word LASSES. Beneath that, is a matchstick man wearing a kilt. There is nothing on the third door, which, I assume is the baby changing area. I cross to the payphone mounted to the tiled wall. Aside from the facilities, there's nothing in here but an arcade machine with a NOT IN SERVICE notice taped to the monitor. An empty, disused vending machine stands like a sentinel in the corner. Posters advertise the times and dates of last year's events. The little enclosure smells of urine and disinfectant. Once again, I revisit my teenage years at a rock concert in my old town hall. Stacks of empty cardboard crates block much of the rear end.

I scoop that handful of coinage the barman from the Black Sun had given me from my pocket, and with droplets of rain dripping from my chin, I dial my local cab firm. As I'm waiting for a dial tone, I hear the baby changing door open behind me. Footsteps approach but I refuse to turn and face them. The phone rings once in my ear.

"Excuse me, mister; have you seen my Daddy?"

I turn towards the source of that strange and unearthly voice, the phone still pressed to the side of my face, already knowing *who* I am going to see before I have even laid eyes on her. That Chinese woman! It's *got* to be! The phone rings twice, three times, then the receiver drops from my slick grip and cracks loudly against the wall. The steel cable attaching the receiver defies gravity and stops the black handle from hitting the ground. It swings in the air like some kind of deranged bungee jumper. I take an uneasy step backwards, turn around and almost fall onto my arse. Fingernails sink into my cheeks as I clutch the sides of my face in horror. My Lord…it's *horrendous*!

From the café, I can hear that cackling hen party laughing mockingly.

"My God," I shudder, looking around for something to defend myself with. "What *are* you?"

Thunder slams two planks of deafening noise together. Rain dribbles through a hole in the roof of the café and pitter-patters against the floor rhythmically. The...*thing* lumbering in front of me can only be described as something that would most feel at home molesting and invading the dreams of the Cthulhu. Poetic as this may sound, it belongs in the corner of an abattoir; coiled in blood and sawdust or lurking in the darkness of the London Underground or perhaps withering and grinding in a disused house, revelling in its own filth and semen.

At first, nothing seems out of the ordinary. It's just a mother and her baby. Nothing untoward here. The baby is naked aside from a nappy strapped around its waist. The mother is wearing a dress...a white dress...dotted with red roses...and that's when I see it-

-oh, good, God-

-they have the wrong *heads*!

The mother's body has the overly large, hairless head of a new-born baby. Its mouth is open. Is it *smiling*? I can see smooth gums revealing white humps that remind me of stepping-stones. It's midway through cutting its *teeth*! Big, harmless, blue eyes gaze down at me, unblinking.

My heart is pounding in my chest as I look down at the chubby arms and legs of a baby that has yet to find its feet. Tiny fingers curl and stretch. I know I shouldn't look, but I am no longer in control of my own actions. I look at its face. It's the Chinese woman! And there's no doubt that this fucking monstrosity is *smiling*! The woman I saw on the train! The woman who had followed me to the Black Sun and cracked the window! She's here now! Her face, her *head*, on the body of a baby that has yet to see its first birthday!

The enormous inflatable head seems to be too big for the spindly neck. It wobbles back and forth like a loose tooth in an infected gum. I want to be sick. I want to shut my eyes and bleach my memory. Scrub it clean with a wire brush if need be! I want to forget. But I can't! How the hell *can* I? I open my mouth to speak but what is there to say? And which one would I even speak to anyhow?

I back off towards the door leading into the café when that humungous wobbly head mumbles, "Mister, have you seen my Daddy?"

Fumbling fingers twist the door handle. I push it open, staggering drunkenly into the café. Bile is greasing the back of my throat. I'm going to vomit. I *want* to vomit! The Italian chef glances up, cocking an eyebrow. "Everything okay?"

I shake my head and try to speak, but it feels like forensics have dusted my gullet. I point towards the door, making a retching noise.

"Did you find the phone?"

"Yeah, I—I…I found it."

"Are you okay?"

"I'm fine. I just need to get out of here."

I run past the cyclist and barge through the beaded curtain, ignoring the wolf whistles and jeering from the pack of fetid women. Stumbling gratefully into the pouring rain, I allow the vomit to rush up my throat, spilling free of my mouth, smacking the pavement. I double over as the landslide of marinated swill pools in front of my feet. I spit mouthfuls of putrid saliva onto the ground, hawking loudly, falling against the window of the café and looking through teary eyes at the church on the opposite side of the road.

CHAPTER 7

I'm surprised to find the church open at this time of night. I squint up through the falling rain at the clock embedded halfway up the rain-saturated edifice. The arch-shaped front door is wide open and I can hear the bells at the rear end of the church tolling. Who would be ringing the bells at such a late hour? It's just gone nine o'clock! I climb the three steps leading into the graveyard and jog up the ramp the disabled parishioners use to enter the church.

The heels of my shoes echo throughout the interior of the church as I pass through the entrance. It looks like nobody is here, but *somebody* must be ringing those bells. I carry on, stepping on the dusty carpet running the length of the aisle, trodden threadbare by thousands of brides over the years. I flop down on one of the wooden pews and allow my head to loll—not *wobble*! From the bottom of the aisle, I can hear someone playing choir music. It must be coming from a CD player in the vestry, which feeds the speakers in here. It's comfortable. It's soothing. I close my eyes and try not to see that horrifically disfigured *thing* behind tightly closed lids. It feels like I'm drunk and the room is spinning. I think I am going to be sick again. Oh no, not in here-

"Good evening."

The voice invades my reverie and I snap my eyes open, searching but fearing what they will reveal. My first dreaded thought is that *thing* from the café backroom has followed me across the road and into the church, but then I look from left to right and find a vicar with a mop of grey hair sitting beside me. I gasp audibly, jumping out of my seat *and* skin!

It's an old wreck of a building. Open doors are liaising with the draughty old windows to make the atmosphere chillier than it should be. Wrought iron radiators mount the walls, but they look older than Hugh Heffner's midwife, and I doubt they would be turned on at such a late hour. When I breathe, a speech bubble of vapour clouds in front of my nose. The church smells of rot and damp, and a chain blocks off the pews overhead with a sign reading CAUTION: RECONSTRUCTION UNDERWAY. They must be replacing all the rotten wood. The whole place looks like it would benefit from a makeover. I glance across to the vicar and try to ignore the gargoyle statue on the wall behind him with the smiling face of a Chinese woman!

"I'm sorry, Father. Am I not meant to be in here?"

"It's perfectly okay."

"I just saw the doors open and…"

The vicar nods his head slowly and folds his arms over his bulging girth. When he smiles at me, I can see his teeth are the colour of lemon peel. His eyes are wide and bloodshot; tufts of grey hair peek from around his ears. He's wearing dark trousers, a purple shirt with his dog collar slipped into place, and he reminds me of somebody—ah, yes, the oldest Klopek brother out of that Tom Hanks movie!

"I hope I'm not disturbing you, Father."

"No, of course not. Anyhow, who am I to dictate when somebody can and cannot converse with Him?" His eyes roll heavenwards.

I smile politely and stand up. "No, you don't understand, Father. I didn't come here to pray. I'm not even religious."

"Yet in your darkest hour you find yourself in His house of worship?"

"Look, I probably should just—"

Freezing cold fingers lock around my elbow. The vicar pulls me gently back—not forcibly—and all of a sudden, emotion overcomes me. A boulder has grown in my throat; replacing my Adam's apple.

"You look as though you need help. What are you running from?"

I refuse to look at the vicar and instead study the vivid reds, yellows, blues, and greens of the stained glass. The things I have seen tonight—the train conductor, Smithy, the old timers, the hen party, the switched-headed monstrous beast and, of course, that stealth Chinese bitch—I should be prepared for anything. But I'm not. And when I see the stained windows depicting a crucified Chinese woman— still fucking *smiling*—I laugh high-pitched, allowing it to roar from my stomach and ripple up my throat. I clap my hands and stomp my feet. Fair game to the vicar—I must look like a right crazy bastard yet he sits patiently until I begin to regain my composure.

"Are you in trouble with the law?"

I shake my head. "Not since I was caught shoplifting a fountain pen from Smith's as a teenager."

"Do you owe somebody money?"

"Yeah," I chuckle childishly. "I owe Smith's £1.99."

The choir music makes a terrible scratching noise; sounding like a flecking dog. In fact, it sounds as though a DJ has dragged the point of a needle across a vinyl record, then that same song from the pub—Love and Marriage, Frank Sinatra—begins flowing through the speakers. I frown across to the vicar who is still watching me. He doesn't seem surprised by the change in music so I ask him about it. He clears his throat and offers me that creepy smile.

"Doesn't everybody love like a bit of old Frank?"

I nod my head and walk out of the row of pews. "I'd better get a move on." The vicar stands up too and extends his hand. I accept the gesture and we shake briefly. "It was nice to meet you, Father."

"Likewise, but before you leave, would you allow me to give you a little advice?"

"Like I said, Father, I'm not religious."

"And neither is my advice."

"Okay."

"Don't keep running. You need to *confront* your fear."

"Father, no offence, but you have no idea—"

"I know you are a lost soul at the moment. And I'm fearful for you."

"I'm fine, Father. I just need to find a taxi—"

"*Listen to her*!" the vicar bellows unexpectedly into my face. His voice relays around the entire church. Flames on burning candles flicker in fear, it seems. "*She's trying to speak to you*!"

"Who is?"

"You *know* who!"

"You're talking out of the back of your head."

"Stop *running* away!"

I walk quickly towards the open doors, the vicar at my side like a bunny-boiling ex-girlfriend. Like that fucking *Nadine*! I clamour down the ramp and back into the downpour. The vicar stops in the doorway.

"Keep running and you will never discover what she wants!" The vicar's booming voice follows me around the corner of the church; barraging through the howling wind. In fact, I can still hear it echoing inside of my head as I run around the back of the church, rain pelting my face.

At the back of this old crumbling wreck, there is a stretch of long grass and stinging nettles. They reach so high that they would happily prickle my waist if I were to go wading in there. This is a church, for crying out loud! Who is in charge of the maintenance of this place? No doubt the worthless council! Useless pricks! You'd have thought that old relic, the vicar, would have coughed up out of his own pocket for a gardener. They earn a packet, so I hear. There's a stonewall framing the church, made slippery from rain and moss. I start towards it, intending to scramble over, but then I see her—The Chinese Woman—standing on the opposite side of the wall amongst an overhanging canopy of soaking wet fern leaves. My face drains of colour; turning the pale shade of eggshells. I stop running, doubling-over, hands on knees, breathing ragged, my eyes fixed on that smiling oddity.

"What do you want from me?" I shriek at her. "Why won't you leave me alone?"

"Oi, you little prick, fuck off now!"

I spin on my heel, caught off guard by the sound of that other voice, and see a bald man wearing a leather jacket, really laying into a youth with a plank of wood. The youngster curls up in a foetal position as the bald man beats seven shades of the brown stuff out of him. I don't know what the poor kid has done to deserve such a brutal beating, but his nose is bleeding badly. In fact, it looks broken. He is holding his ribs as the bald fellah whacks him another three times with the wood. The weapon looks like a table leg.

I back away, eager not to get involved. The bald man steps forward, holding that blood-smeared plank towards me. "Don't be a hero, dickhead. Just keep walking."

"I…you need…" I glance across at the curled up youth on his knees, coughing, spluttering, and sobbing. He's drenched with both rain and blood. Wind howls like a cackling madman. "Are you okay, mate?"

"He's fine," the bald man barks. "Now do one!"

I glance over at the Chinese woman. She has stepped from underneath the tree and has approached the wall. I don't think either the hairless man or his victim have seen her. "I wasn't talking to you," I shout. When I swallow, it feels like blended glass has commingled with my saliva. Hands shake uncontrollably.

"This little cunt owes me two grand," the bald man confesses. "The fucker didn't come forward when we held his *son* hostage! Not even when we removed his big toe! He's a coward! A little fucking shit stain! Little bastard would sell his own mother for a hit! Now, if you still want to help him, I suggest you either get your wallet out or keep walking!"

"You don't have to beat him."

"And you don't have to get involved."

I look over to the Chinese woman. She has started walking away from the church, following the wet stretch of grass leading towards a nest of trees and bushes. She turns and waves at me, still smiling. I look down at that beaten youth and realise there is nothing I can do for him. If he is indeed a junkie, or he owes the yob money, then there's little I can do to help. It's his own problem. I've already taken one hammering tonight. I certainly don't intend on going one-on-one against this maniac. I mumble something of an apology to the bleeding youth and then sprint towards the Chinese woman, climbing over that pistachio-coloured wall. She is waving at me and it's then that I realise she is holding her hand out for me. I look back over my shoulder, knowing I should help the youth, but also knowing I am powerless. I wish there was something I could do. I wish I could help him. But I can't. The only thing I would achieve would be getting the *both* of us beaten. Maybe even *murdered.*

I trod through the soaking wet grass, ignoring the thorns snagging my trousers; ignoring the nettles tingling my legs; ignoring the pouring rain, stopping in front of the Chinese woman. She's still offering me her small hand. Slowly, I raise my own and wrap my fingers around hers. I can feel the beat of my heart quicken. My mouth becomes bone dry. I feel electricity pumping through my body, tingling the fillings in my teeth, making my bowels loosen, my stomach churn.

And then we both hit the ground, huddled beside one another, still holding hands, still staring into each other's eyes...

looking...

at...

...

CHAPTER 8

... the floor. Wood effect linoleum. Baby blue walls decorated with canvas pictures of flowers, beaches with a silhouetted lighthouse in the background, forests dotted with bluebells, a couple of Banksy classics. There's a TV playing in the background. Can't see it but I can hear it. Where the fuck am I? I look down at my feet and realise that not only am I high above the ground, but my toe nails are painted red. A few torrid seconds later, and I realise I am standing at the peak of a stepladder. A leather recliner sofa is perched in the corner of the room.

I'm getting scared now. More frightened with each passing second—even more petrified when the acrylic fingernails on my right hand grab a knotted noose hanging from the ceiling. What the hell am I doing*? What the hell is* going *on?*

And then I drop from the ladder.

No pain.

No gasping. No flailing.

The neck has not broken. No doubt about that. I can see myself—no, not me, it's not me*—and I'm swaying. Swinging. I look down, no restrictions here, and when I do, I can see the belly is swollen, not pouchy, but shapely.*

Pregnant!

I can hear gagging, retching, the TV again. No, it's not a TV, it's a stereo, a song—a Frank Sinatra song! No, not this again! Anything but this!

And then it all makes sense to me.

This isn't me!

I'm not the one dying!

I am not the person hanging!

Nadine is!

A pregnant Nadine!

As Love and Marriage plays on, I watch helplessly as her legs thrash out, knocking CD's and trinkets from a shelf, those strangled gurgling noises now beginning to fade. And then I realise her glazed eyes have fell upon a dog-eared poster seollotaped to a closed door opposite. There's a smiling face on the crinkled paper, one of those acid, round, bright yellow smiling face…

…

CHAPTER 9

I wake with a constipated gasp, rubbing sleep-encrusted eyes with the ball of my palm. I jump back in my seat, head bouncing off the sponge headrest, and notice that I'm back on the train—*the* train—the same damn train. It's just about to depart from the station and my mobile phone is ringing, filling the carriage with The Match of the Day theme. As I pull it out of my pocket, a snickering pack of cackling women step on the train; passing around a bottle of bright green alchopop. They're wearing pink cowgirl Stetson's and denim belts for skirts. I glance down at the name on the screen of my phone and see the name NADINE displayed. I thumb the connect button and wedge the phone between my jaw and ear.

"Nadine, are you okay?"

"Yes, but, this…this is a little difficult, I…I *really* need to talk to you."

"I know. Are you home?"

A fibrous man with a bright purple Mohawk shoulders past me, grunting something of an apology.

Spencer Rogers smiles up from the seat opposite, chowing on a sandwich, flashing rotten teeth and mashed cheese and onion.

"Yes, I'm at the flat," her sweet voice fills my ear.

"Can I come over?"

A strangled sob. I hear her voice crack. She's crying.

"Please," she sniffs. "Do you remember where I live?"

I nod and make my way to the doors of the train. I step onto the platform, noticing the rank of restocked taxis opposite the motionless locomotive. "Berrywood, right?"

"Yes. That's correct." Nadine breathes into the canal of my ear.

"I'll be right over." I slip my phone into the pocket of my coat and move away from the train. Just before the doors close and lock, the nasal-congested voice of Spencer Rogers blurts "See you Monday, mate."

Smiling genuinely, I wave at Spencer. "See you Monday, *mate.*"

***

BIOGRAPHY

James Jobling has been a rabid fan of anything horror for most of his life, blaming his older brother for leaving a copy of James Herbert's fantastic novel, *The Rats*, lounging around the living room when he was only a child for starting his obsession. A huge fan of the horror book genre, he regards James Herbert and David Moody as his writing heroes - with the latter being his inspiration for getting into writing. *National Emergency* is James's first book.

He lives in Manchester, England, with his world – his beautiful wife, two adorable, sleep-avoiding children, and Nanook, his pet beagle. He can be contacted through Facebook and would be honored to hear from anybody who might wish to get in touch. Also, please visit www.thebackroadbooks.com to join the BRB mailing list. No Spam, ever. We promise. Only random news and the occasional free book

Printed in Great Britain
by Amazon